WASHITA

Weird Custer

A Novel

By William Sumrall

Washita Weird Custer is a work of historical fiction. Apart from the well-known actual people, events, and locales that figure in the narrative, all names, characters, places, and incidents are the products of the author's imagination or are used fictitiously. Any resemblance to current events or locales, or to living persons, is entirely coincidental.

SHANTI PUBLISHING

Shanti Publishing
PO Box 6252
Pine Mountain Club, CA 93222

www.ShantiPublishing.com

Acknowledgements

To James VerDoorn; a most excellent artist - thank you for graciously allowing the use of your magnificent digital painting for the cover of this book. To Audrey Balliett; thank you for your honest opinions about style and what you liked - and didn't like. To Jennifer Farmer; thank you for your insight into Native American customs and rituals.

Table of Contents

Chapter One: Halcyon Days

It was during those heady, halcyon days long after the flowers had turned to fruit on the wild plum trees, that they came.

The verdure of prairie grasses carpeted the Southern Plains like a sheening, iridescent sea of emerald beneath the cerulean sky. The bucolic setting was redefined however, in a violent interfusion of sanguinary brush strokes.

It was a masterpiece of aberration; an opus magnus of insanity. It was like the work of some Spanish pastoral painter whose mind was ablaze – consumed in the tertiary stage of an unspeakable affliction. It was the work of an artist gone mad - attacking the canvas with his brushes.

These were the hot, humid days of August; days which cooled like a killed carcass and presaged the blood red, scarlet cloaking of the trees of autumn. Murder and rapine washed in a tsunami over the plains. It was as though an overfilled blood vat had been upended and released its sanguinous contents onto the floor of a slaughter house.

On they came, in howling, lethal, mounted assault waves of 5,000 to 10,000 painted braves. They were led by shirtless, sun tanned, thickly muscled chiefs. These were chiefs who wore double trailered war bonnets of eagle feathers, and whose shining bodies were painted in magical icons of fearsome sorcery.

On they came, to the very fringes of Fort Leavenworth, Kansas. No settler was safe in the path of the crimson tide from Texas to New Mexico. Nor were they safe from Colorado through the Oklahoma Indian Territory and to the north, into the Dakotas and the Montana Territory.

They were like dispossessed, fearsome tenants who had come to lay claim to what was formerly theirs.

Logistics and concern for necessities did not undermine the tempestuous thoughts of those men who rode the painted ponies. Men, whose abstract minds raged behind the piceous eyes of their tattooed faces. These were visages masked in the pigments of charcoal and ocher, of bird excrement, berries, saliva and buffalo fat.

The marauding war parties had accrued knowledge of the location of permanent bodies of water. And through hundreds of years of internecine warfare, they'd learned to subsist spontaneously from the land and through plunder.

The seasonal red juggernaut rolled over the land like a ravenous, seething body of painted locusts. It left behind it a desolate wasteland.

Pillars of smoke, from the burned-out ruins of thousands of homesteads, rose in columns high into the sky. Wrecked dreams, shattered in a metal storm of bullets bore witness to the release of pent up vengeance.

The queues of gray-black smoke resembled the flesh fueled vapors from Old Testament sacrifices as they ascended vertically, merging with and vanishing into the billowing white cumulus clouds. The alabaster formations resembled mounted braves and scudded ominously across the ocean blue sky at six thousand feet.

But the raging fires were not offerings to the white man's god. They were instead sacrifices to the arcane gods of the painted men who sang with tattooed faces lifted to the sky – a rifle in one hand and a bottle of whiskey in the other.

They danced the scalp dance around the roaring conflagrations. They burned white men at the stake while taking their women as warbrides and children to be raised as their own.

These were men who had, in the space of one hundred years, been transplanted from the stone-age and pitted against men of the industrial age. It was a mismatch in an unequal fight to the death.

These dangerous men, so displaced in time, also sought warbrides, women with whom to take unto themselves as wives. They sought to augment their plummeting numbers in a last-ditch attempt to avoid irrelevance.

On the isolated farms, the large families of European American settlers watched in alarm as the gray-black columns of smoke ascended inexorably into the atmosphere. The explanation of which could be heard whispered in the murmurs carried on the hot, dry wind of the Southern Plains – distant gun fire.

Faint and barely perceptible, the popping sound of musketry foretold of the fate that was rolling like a massive engine of retribution in their direction. Some settlers fled, and wisely so. But most remained and fought like infantry until they were shot, cut down, and their women taken.

Once the seasonal thrusts had climaxed into an abhorrent orgasm, it retrograded to its nexus. It receded as a devastating seasonal flood recedes home to its riverbanks and resumes its determined, irresistible course.

"Into this maelstrom of fire, I will send the Boy General," exclaimed the insane President Andrew Johnson.

The president did not fit the image of what one in such an esteemed office would be expected to reflect. He was of medium height and powerfully built. He had the body of a prize fighter and the face of a killer;

he was in fact, known to kill – quiet often and with very little provocation.

"I am of an aim to quash this seasonal invasion of painted assassins," the seventeenth president paused in his monologue.

He paused while he massaged the lower left side of his back with a tan, liver spotted hand. The president rubbed at the sharp pain that plagued his kidney – yet another of the incessant, relentless kidney stones that dogged him.

The thick fingers of his fleshy right hand tightened around the neck of an amber bottle of Tennessee bourbon. Its contents were vaguely visible and ill-defined as the POTUS tilted the half empty bottle bottoms up. President Johnson began chugging it, his Adam's apple rising and falling like a piston. He swallowed hard until he was sure the fiery liquid was all gone.

"Damn, that hit the spot!" President Johnson exclaimed to himself. He wiped his mouth with the back of his right forearm, like a man.

"I am chosen by God to be the President of the United States! I am the sword hammered from the plow shear by the God Almighty Himself to smite the heathen hordes; these nomadic bands that assail good, God fearing Christian folk! These are marauding gangs of mass murderers who seek to challenge my authority! Authority which was given by *God Himself!*

"It is I, Andrew Johnson, who has been appointed by the Almighty to protect His flock. I will unleash my dark sword and set right the course of this river of vile putrescence that has maligned my frontiers these days of late!

"In the months that come, I will dispatch my *Destroyer Angel* unto a mission of death, as the good Lord doth intend, for He is a vengeful Lord, and *I will send my Angel with a blood-stained sword*!" rambled president Johnson, sincere in what he was saying.

Thirty armed blacks – gigantic Negro soldiers stood restlessly as the President of the United States raged on. The president seemed to focus his bleary, jaundiced eyes at some imaginary figure in the spacious room that only he, himself could see.

Without warning, President Johnson whirled 180 degrees and faced his retinue of uniformed bodyguards. All of them were hand-picked Medal of Honor recipients from the recent Civil War. The sclera of their eyes beamed from their shiny, ebony faces as the president ranted. Their pulses galloped with the killing lust that this man invoked among them.

"'How would you die, General Custer?' I asked the Boy General in a vision I had," rambled the schizophrenic, bipolar seventeenth President of the United States.

The sweat pores on Johnson's overlarge nose, made cauliflowered by years of alcoholism, were accentuated and made prominent by the urgent sputtering of the whale oil lanterns that augmented the gas lights. The lanterns cast a soft, steady yellow light over his unhealthy skin.

"'*DEATH BY COMBAT!*' the *Prodigal Son* answered me," President Johnson exclaimed to his Negro troops, in his thick, hybrid Carolina-Tennessee accent.

At this exclamation, a monstrously built former slave and soldier-hero shouted an order. This man wore the Medal of Honor and was the sergeant major of the hand-picked soldiers. He led the men that often surrounded the paranoid, violence prone President Andrew Johnson.

The sergeant major shouted to his soldiers who all wore dress blue uniforms of parade, and they repeated, shouting in lusty unison:

"UM! UMGAWA! JOHNSON GOT THUH POWAH! UM! UMGAWA! JOHNSON GOT THUH POWUH! UM! UMGAWA JOHNSON..."

Chapter Two: Conclave of Generals

"My cavalry is stretched, and by force of necessity cannot ride naked and unencumbered as do the Cheyenne, Sioux and their Arapaho accomplices," complained General Phillip "Little Phil" Sheridan to his superior, General William Tecumseh Sherman.

"Once their appetite has been appeased, they take their captives and disperse in sundry directions, converging at some nebulous, preconceived rendezvous hundreds of miles distant. It is there," continued Sheridan, "that they barter for and parley amongst themselves, selecting brides with which to add sum to their numbers."

Sallow faced and unshaven, General Sherman contemplated the import of Little Phil's frank assessment. His face had not seen a razor in days and was covered in a rough stubble of gray shadowed with red.

"So, you think that the rumors are true," responded Sherman, "they believe they face extinction unless they can get their numbers up."

Little Phil regarded Sherman easily, responding to his fellow general officer with an open air of familiarity.

"Yes," replied Little Phil, explaining, "half of their population was obliterated through a series of cholera outbreaks in the late 1840s, and they never recovered from it. Add to that small pox, influenza, and a plethora of other maladies, not to mention their violent nature – which in itself is not conducive to longevity."

Almost dwarfish in stature, General Sheridan enviously regarded the height of the lanky, disheveled General Sherman who stood at six feet tall. Sherman was standing in front of a map of the United States which had been tacked onto the unstained, rough-hewn walls made of oak plank.

Sheridan's attention was temporarily drawn from Sherman as a buckboard wagon wheeled noisily by outside. The driver began cursing as he laid the whip onto the back of the sweating mule.

Known as "Cump" to his friends, Sherman presented a scruffy, unclean appearance that hinted at, and suggested his underlying personality. Red, thinning hair presided atop a broad forehead that shielded a brain of great complexity and enormous intelligence. The disheveled hair always appeared unwashed and oily.

"Maybe I need a bath," Cump thought to himself, as he scratched at what he thought might be a flea, "but everyone knows that bathing leads to pneumonia."

Personal hygiene was not an earmark of the general any more than carrying a comb.

Beneath the heavy eyebrows, dark brown irises seemed to meld into the black pupils of the too closely set, weasel like eyes of Sherman.

"The eyes of a ferret," smiled General Sheridan to himself, while he ruminated over the lethal nature of the man in front of him. Sheridan knew full well how Sherman had coined the term, "Total War." And within that knowledge resided dark secrets of evil unfathomed.

Phillip Sheridan was a strikingly small man, who wore special cavalry boots with elevated insoles. No one knew about the elevated insoles, but they made Little Phil appear to stand nearly four feet eleven inches, nudging five feet.

"President Johnson is breathing down my neck to set Custer loose," said Sherman to his friend.

"He is adamant about stopping these seasonal depredations, and between you and me, I'll let you in on a little secret – the president has gone crazy," confided Sherman.

"They've been taking women in these raids for two generations," continued Sherman, who added with emphasis, "*warbrides!* It's not like it just started this morning! But Johnson is making a big deal out of it all of a sudden. The Cheyenne are causing a big headache, taking all of these warbrides – plainly so."

Sheridan answered reflexively, almost before Sherman had completed his statement, "And that's the only thing that has offset their catastrophic infant mortality rate."

General Sheridan explained to Sherman what he already knew, "The Caucasian women have an inherited resistance to the plethora of maladies afflicting the Cheyenne, and the white women have a much higher fecundity rate."

"That is the only reason they have not been quashed into extinction," replied Sherman.

"They are becoming bigger, stronger – through the abduction of warbrides. Hybrids. Practically all of them tower over six feet in stature. And those bastards are strong too," Sherman added, "muscular as hell!"

The assessment came from thin, downturned lips that seldom formed a smile. Suddenly, without warning, Sherman sneezed, and then taking his thumb and index finger placed them to his long, straight nose and blew hard.

General Sherman paced the wooden floor and the peculiar officer continued talking as he wiped his nose with the sleeve of his double breasted, fourteen button frock coat. The gold colored buttons stood out against the wool frock coat, dyed to a dark Navy blue.

"But I have a plan. Come here, Phil. I want to show you something," said Sherman to his colleague, leading him into the adjacent room. Sherman walked with a straight carriage. Sheridan swung toward the room bow legged and gnome-like from years in the saddle.

Little Phil waddled like a chimpanzee, and as he followed the taller man, he could not help but feel repugnance at the lingering bouquet of odor that always surrounded General Sherman.

There, on a pedestal stood an object the height of a man, and it was shrouded beneath a white cotton linen sheet. The object beneath the linen was inanimate. Sherman stood facing it, and turned his head suddenly toward Little Phil. His thin, scrawny neck was hidden by the high, upturned collar of the white three button pull over shirt beneath his frock coat.

"Watch this," said Sherman to the dwarfish man who had followed him into the room. Suddenly, Sherman savagely ripped the linen sheet from the figure.

Little Phil stood amazed at the life like figure of George Armstrong Custer standing atop the dais. The apparition was dressed in cavalry regalia, standing with feet apart and looking straight ahead with its arms folded across its chest. There was something uncanny about the artistically made, sculpture like figure that filled the small man with unease.

"What's the meaning of this?" asked Sheridan, the apprehension in his voice was palpable.

18

General Sherman at first did not answer, but instead depressed a foot pedal at the base of the dais and set it into a slow, revolving motion.

"West Point. Class of 1861. *Combat model!*" Sherman's voice had deepened and carried with it the tone of authority. Suddenly Sherman shifted his monolog into high gear and infused enthusiasm into his martial homily, "You haven't seen anything yet, Phil – *it kills!*"

"Nice," responded Little Phil Sheridan.

"The combat series Custer will kill when I depress this foot lever – like this!" exclaimed Sherman, who turned his head to face his fellow officer, and grinned for the first time.

Sheridan could see why Sherman seldom parted his lips affably; the stained, crowded ivories that smiled back at him were in an advanced state of dental decay.

With the rotation of the dais upon which the figure stood, a revolving cylinder began plucking the teeth of a steel comb, generating the musical melody, *Gary Owen*.

At the sound of this lively Irish tavern tune, the Custer combat model came to life hesitantly. It began turning its head in measured, jerky motions to stare into the face of Little Phil Sheridan in a pantomime manner.

"What unseemly manner of mechanics is this!" demanded General Sheridan, clearly taken aback. Sheridan's palms were sweating, and he felt increasingly ill at ease.

"Just be still and watch, it will kill," placated Cump Sherman, "just watch."

"Kill what? Who?" postulated General Phillip Sheridan.

The dais continued its melodic rotation until the Custer combat series was facing Sheridan again.

The inspiring, barroom melody from the musical drum continued, and the life like figure of Custer stepped off the dais in jerking, robotic half movements. It advanced on the uneasy four-foot, eleven-inch spectator.

Suddenly the gauntleted hands of the Custer thing seized Sheridan fiercely by his bull neck.

"Help! I have been set upon!" shouted the general, twisting his thick, corded neck and contorting his reddened face into a visage of consummate consternation.

"Get it off of me, Cump!!!" reiterated Little Phil, through coughs and gasps.

Suddenly the Custer figure began laughing, releasing General Sheridan and walking to the pine knotted wall to lean on for support as he laughed hysterically.

General Sherman was bent double, slapping his knees and gasping for air. He was laughing so hard that the veins distended upon his reddened, pronounced forehead.

"Now, that's entertainment!" laughed the Boy General, taking in a deep breath of air.

"My stomach muscles hurt from laughing so hard that I feel like I did fifty sit-ups!" exclaimed Custer.

Chapter Three: The Plan

Major General Phillip H. Sheridan commanded the Department of the Missouri, a massive 400,000 square mile land mass which included Kansas, the Oklahoma Indian Territory, New Mexico and Colorado.

One of the most isolated and western most forts that thrust into the Kansas frontier was Fort Dodge, a critical stopover for westward bound wagon trains. It was an expansive complex, sprawling about one hundred acres and consisting in part of block houses made of quarried stone. The buildings were set apart in such a way as to provide the mutual support of interlocking fields of fire against the incessant Indian attacks.

It was here at Fort Dodge located on the Santa Fe Trail which connected Independence, Missouri with Santa Fe, New Mexico that Generals Sherman, Sheridan, and Lieutenant Colonel Custer discussed the "Indian Problem" that plagued the enormous geographical expanse of the Department of the Missouri.

The physically diminutive Sheridan, with his small and scattered army, had not been able to cope with the robust aggressiveness of the Indians during the raiding season. So, he had set up a tenuous, nearly impotent defense. He did the best with what he had.

A screen of distant, remote military forts constructed of heavy timber protected the frontier settlements. Undermanned cavalry patrols consisting of up to twenty individuals moved beyond the far-flung forts in blind attempts to intercept the Indians. This defensive policy was only partially successful.

Major George A. Forsyth's desperate stand at Beecher's Island on the Arickaree in northeastern Colorado dealt the Cheyenne a heavy blow. Major E.A. Carr's expedition in the Republican River country put to flight a large band of bronco Cheyenne on the prowl, preventing the acquisition of hundreds of warbrides. But despite these and other limited successes, reports from the frontier were ominous; there was an enormous gathering of tribes in the Oklahoma Indian Territory.

On August 17th, 1868 the balding and prematurely aged Governor Crawford of Kansas, telegraphed the paranoid, unpredictable President Johnson demanding that action be taken.

Distance had given a coward's courage to Crawford's bold rhetoric. Had Crawford been within arm's reach of Johnson, he would not have dared to speak to this particular president in so foolish a way.

Returning to the main topic, Sheridan explained his problem to the lanky, disheveled General Sherman as Custer listened carefully.

Sheridan did not ignore the Boy General and was cognizant of how alive Custer's blue eyes were, in comparison to the cold, dead, graphite eyes of Sherman. But the three men were of a type; even a casual observer could feel with the innate intuition that all people are born with, that these three men were seasoned killers.

There was a common martial thread that tied off the umbilical cord at birth with these three. This was a triumvirate of war lords who lusted for the clash of arms, the clash of cultures, and the overpowering desire to perform their "warrior's ritual" on a scale reminiscent of Caesar's invasion of Gaul.

"With my army scattered across an expanse of 400,000 miles, I can't be at the right place at the right time during the raiding season," complained Sheridan.

"What I've tried to do," Sheridan explained, "is set up a screen of forts to protect the settlements. The garrison commanders run patrols, but these are in the main, insufficient, and have proven to be wanting. Forsyth's stand at Beecher's Island and Custer's killing of Roman Nose has helped, along with other isolated rabbit punches, such as Major Carr's expedition into the Republican River country."

24

Sheridan paused in his monologue in order to access an object from a black leather kit, a sort of medical satchel that doctors carry. From it he procured a one pint, brown colored glass bottle containing laudanum. With effort he was partially able to obfuscate the trembling of his pudgy hands.

By the time of the Victorian Era, the use of laudanum had become widespread. Touted as a "cure all," it was even spooned to choleric infants to calm them. The common ratio to proportion was 10% opium to 90% alcohol. But there was no standard and the ratio to proportion often had a broader range.

"Cump, get me your whiskey. George, I know you don't indulge, so pay me no mind," stated General Sheridan to his colleagues. There was an edge to his voice he couldn't hide as he fought to control it.

"I can't drink this neat, Cump," Sheridan added.

In fact, he could drink the laudanum undiluted, but he found the opium alkaloids to be extremely bitter, but when diluted with strong spirits, he was less inclined to become nauseated.

General Sherman poured four ounces of Tennessee bourbon into a beautiful glass rummer. It was cut with a band of waisted panels on a fluted, spreading stem. The vessel was round footed, and tinted translucent blue from the absurdly high lead content. He handed the rummer, half full to Sheridan, who accepted the ornate rummer anxiously.

Carefully, General Sheridan poured an oversized shot of laudanum into the bourbon and swirled the mixture with his forefinger. Then he raised the glass to his small, petite mouth, trying not to spill the contents with his tremulous hand. The powerful elixir burned its way through his mouth, down his throat and into his stomach.

"Governor Crawford has gone over my head and telegraphed President Johnson," complained Sheridan, "Crawford did not exaggerate of the horrific and growing number of Indian massacres occurring daily. If that were not bad enough, so has Governor Hall of Colorado.

"I am furious with the chiefs of these Cheyenne, Arapaho and Sioux tribes who continue standing idly by and are allowing this to transpire. It reminds me of fathers who can't *OR WILL NOT CONTROL THEIR UNRULY SONS!*

"As it stands, President Johnson is breathing down my neck and threatening to reduce me to the ranks. *He may replace me if I can't get the situation under control!*" exclaimed Little Phil.

"I have anticipated your needs, Phil" reassured Sherman, eyeing the bottle of laudanum thoughtfully as he tilted his bottle of bourbon, pulling a large swig and swirling it in his mouth, feeling it sting his receded, infected gum line. He did not wince, as other men might have.

"I propose a winter campaign; a saber thrust into the Valley of the Washita!" erupted Little Phil like a pent-up volcano – he was able to speak more freely as the tincture of opium relaxed his train of thought. He was feeling better now – a lot better.

The Irish brogue he had picked up from his immigrant parents became pronounced, and startling clear. He was ashamed of his Irish ancestry and tried to suppress the brogue. Yet it became more pronounced as the tincture loosened his tongue.

"Early in August, I had issued the tribes an annuity of goods, including arms and ammunition as promised at the Medicine Lodge conclave. However," Sheridan continued, "they immediately set themselves to the warpath with the arms provided."

The exclamation came in a rush of angry words. These words were spoken in acrimony through the tightened lips of man who disdained regulated warfare, and loathed arming up his adversaries, whom he knew would use the rifles to kill his soldiers.

"Well, of course, Phil. I know about all of that. But on the other hand, I have anticipated your logistical requirements for a winter campaign," replied Sherman, taking the brown, translucent bottle of laudanum with his right hand and tilting it bottoms up. The powerful, bitter taste caused the Civil War hero to lick his chapped lips.

Sheridan watched Sherman take the large pull off of the pint bottle and didn't like it. He spoke up about it, too, "Easy on that, Cump. Hard to come by sometimes."

"Look," continued General Sherman, "I have spoken at length with Grant on this problem. It was no mean feat to convince him to give you free hand in this matter."

Gradually, the import of what Sherman was saying dawned on Little Phil Sheridan, and he was transformed; he became animated, excited at the portent of Sherman's statement.

"Total war!" responded Little Phil, "A moniker that you coined so well as you laid waste to Georgia."

And laid waste to Georgia Sherman had. What Cump Sherman had done was not lost on any of the three officers present.

Paradoxically, Sherman had been the foster son of a prominent Charleston lawyer and Whig politician and had been popular with the upper crust of the old Southern Aristocracy.

William T. Sherman had not been opposed to slavery, and his sympathy to the institution had been manifested by his refusal to employ Negro troops in his command. Nevertheless, he was virulently opposed to secession.

Enthusiastically, Sherman had murderously ripped the bosom from the breast that had fed him. He led his army with an insatiable blood hunger during his inexorable push into the emaciated underbelly of the starving South.

Sheridan continued expounding the thesis of his doctrinal approach to the incipient winter campaign. "For weeks I have fantasized of making plans for a strong, decisive punitive campaign. All of the aboriginals would be affected. For the following reason -- it is useless to categorize the Indians as friendly or hostile, I mistrust especially those who reneged on the Medicine Lodge Treaties. The chiefs continually blame "bad Injuns" for the atrocities being committed in Kansas and Colorado. I mean to treat the Indians as a single entity and hold their hands to the fire! My strategy of reprisal will be initiated by the onset of winter."

"A winter campaign this far out is almost unprecedented," opined Custer, the nation's foremost cavalry officer, "the logistics of such stratagem are formidable."

Despite the doubt expressed by the Boy General, there was an import of anticipation, of excitement in the tone of Custer's voice – the ebullience of Sheridan's enthusiasm had had the effect of a contagion.

The Boy General went on to collude with Sheridan's opinion, his words carried the weight of knowledge gained through experience, "Their ponies will be emaciated, and of almost no use to them. They will by the force of nature, be confined to their winter sanctuaries, along river valleys, huddled next to their fires within their tepees, immobilized, and denied the advantage of their beasts."

Sherman took another swig of the potent elixir, chasing it with two mouthfuls of bourbon. Unused to opiates, his ears were ringing, and his mouth and face were numb. Looking at Custer, Sherman said, "And that is why I chose *you* to lead the campaign. I *knew* what Sheridan was thinking. I can read his mind. Plus," General Sherman added, "you two were a team during the war. Worked together good. I liked that then and I like it now."

But that was not the entirety of it, Sherman knew. Cump Sherman kept to himself the fact that President Johnson had personally interceded on Custer's behalf, insisting that his personal friend lead the assault elements. Close, personal friends were rare commodities for the president, and Sherman knew not to cross Johnson, who was an unpredictable, dangerous man.

"What about Sully?" queried the Yellow Hair, cognizant and suspicious of the fort commander's equal rank, anticipating a challenge to his authority.

"I need Lieutenant Colonel Sully to coordinate the logistics for the time being," answered Cump Sherman.

"Once the campaign has begun, he will be sent home. He is more conservative in his approach than are you. You'll see. He lacks your panache, but he is a skilled administrator and the logistics include over 400 supply wagons. When he exhibits reticence to close with and destroy the enemy, you will replace him. He will provoke his own transfer to the rear with the gear, rest assured," placated General Sherman.

"Here," offered General Sherman, proffering the half empty bottle of bourbon to the Boy General, "take a sip. Can't hurt anything, man."

"Never," responded the blond, blue eyed lieutenant colonel, politely waving the spirits away. Custer did not drink, did not smoke, and did not chew tobacco. It was also rumored that he did not make love. This was on account of a chronic malady of the most personal nature acquired at a brothel while a cadet at West Point.

Custer's childless marriage often provoked good natured kidding from fellow officers, but behind the smiles were the suspicions that the repugnant rumors which circulated were true.

"I mean to ally myself with the weather," interceded Little Phil, who directed his gaze at Cump Sherman.

"The army," continued Sheridan, "with proper backing from Washington, can transport the required forage and logistics in the wagon trains. I am set on conducting this winter campaign into the Valley of the Washita with Custer at its head. It will be the most formidable winter offensive ever undertaken and will ultimately deliver the coup de grace to the recalcitrant tribes."

"I approve your plan and all details that you will have forthcoming," assured General William Tecumseh Sherman. "President Johnson has through General

Grant afforded me leave to do whatever is necessary to assist you in your endeavor. The acquiescence of the Interior Department is assured," General Sherman added in a relaxed, reassuring tone.

"Very well!" responded Sheridan.

"Then lend me your ears my fellow officers," continued Sheridan, "for there is somewhat more to hear appertaining to my plan. I will utilize the tactics of converging columns. Custer will lead eleven companies of the elite Seventh Cavalry, a battalion of infantry under Major Page, and the Nineteenth Kansas Volunteer Cavalry. This force will establish a huge logistics depot, to be named Camp Supply. Two other columns will thrust into the Oklahoma Indian Territory in concert with Custer's advance.

"Major Evans will march east from Fort Bascom, New Mexico and Major Carr will advance to the southeast from Fort Lyon, Colorado. Once Camp Supply is established, Custer will carry his attack without delay to the tribes all along the Washita River."

"Intriguing," responded Sherman, adding, "how long do you anticipate the duration of the campaign to perdure?"

"Six months," interpolated Custer, "that will keep them reeling and off balance through the entirety of the winter season."

"Vast stores of ammunition and supplies have been accumulating at Fort Dodge, Fort Lyon, Bascom and Arbuckle," elaborated General Sherman.

Sherman was at ease, speaking in his element with the freedom to grant anything he wished. President Johnson had assured the resources of the entire United States if necessary. The generals had not had such a luxury since the Civil War.

"I have anticipated your every need." explained Sherman. The explanation implied an iron clad guarantee that was directed at both of the Army officers.

"My men?" asked Lieutenant Colonel Custer.

"Your men will receive winter clothing. Notable Indian and white scouts are being recruited at this very moment," answered Sherman.

"Among them," Cump Sherman added, "are California Joe, Bloody Knife, Hard Rope and Little Beaver – Bloody Knife is an old friend of yours, so I've heard." Sherman was speaking seriously; there was no import of friendliness implied in the metallic tone of his voice.

The dead, onyx eyes of Sherman, which the newspaper the *Cincinnati Commercial* had called "insane" firmly held the lively, blue eyes of Custer. The Boy General did not blink.

"This is an important task," said Sherman to Custer, adding, "I can see into you…"

"And I can see into *you*," thought the Boy General to himself. Sherman was no coward, Custer knew.

When Confederate General Albert Sydney Johnston had turned on Grant viciously at Shiloh, Sherman's division had been hit full on by a 40,000-man human wave attack launched in the darkness of predawn. Johnston, a psychopathic, suicidal general, had days before received 18,600 British Enfield rifles. The Enfields had been delivered by two English blockade runners. The ships, flying the ensign of the Union Jack had made it through the cordon of Union ships that was strangling the South. These modern rifles augmented a mismatched arsenal of flintlocks, shotguns and farm implements that the hastily assembled rebels were armed with.

In vain, Johnston's subordinates tried to dissuade the "Swords and Roses" General Johnston from launching the doomed, risk-all attack.

"I would fight them," Albert Sydney Johnston had said, "if they were a million!"

The rebel attack force was composed of sharecroppers, farmers and poor whites. It was led by West Point graduates. The barefooted army approached in four columns during the darkness and resembled the antiquated, deep, medieval attack columns of another age. They covered a front of about three miles wide and one mile deep.

The Confederate juggernaut steam rolled over Sherman's forward pickets, causing General Sherman to reel backwards. Wounded twice in the battle – in the shoulder and hand, Cump had controlled the retreat and prevented it from degenerating into a rout. Notwithstanding, he'd had three horses shot out from under him. It was for this reason that the Yellow Hair liked the man.

Chapter Four: Arctic Air Mass

In the mid-autumn of 1868 a series of low pressure, arctic cold air masses had moved into the Great Plains earlier than expected and stalled, lingering and almost halting in place. This out of season, atmospheric phenomena subjected the vast, vulnerable underlying regions to harsh early winter conditions.

By the second week of November 1868, standing bodies of water had frozen and a shimmering twelve-inch quilt of frozen snow blanketed the ice hardened ground in a ghostly white mantel.

It was now, it was here, it was in this opportune moment offered by the Gods of War that Custer would unsheathe President Johnson's dark sword. This Destroyer Angel, this Prodigal Son born to die in combat, this enigma of a man – both admired and vilified - had been sent into the Oklahoma Indian Territory in a quest for the Holy Grail – victory against the Cheyenne!

The Yellow Hair wore a heavy winter coat as he rode at the front of the column mounted on his favorite sorrel gelding, Vic. The thousand-pound Kentucky thoroughbred champed at the bit and stamped at the hoof – eager for action as it led the Seventh Cavalry out of Fort Dodge.

Custer was riding point and relying completely on his compass in the white out conditions. He was an accomplished scout in his own right and expert in land navigation.

The former general was driving his men hard while riding into the blistering cold winds toward the Oklahoma Indian Territory. He was headed in the direction of where Wolf and Beaver Creeks meet and conjoin. It was there in that far flung, little known wilderness that Custer and Sully intended to establish Camp Supply.

But it was on Mulberry Creek that Custer made his first camp, waiting for Lieutenant Colonel Sully to bring up the 400-wagon logistics train.

The Yellow Hair had far less use for the battalion of infantry under Major Page, which was proceeding at a snail's pace and which the Boy General secretly hoped would not arrive in time. Custer was a career cavalry officer and felt that infantry held him up - slowed down his pace.

The wagons were variants of the US Army six mule Wagon-Model 1858. Many had the upgraded running gear modifications applied in 1864. The wagons were rated a payload of 2,000 pounds.

The Kansas volunteers had been ambushed by Cheyenne multiple times and were continually harried by the wolf skinned men as they fought for their lives on their way toward the Yellow Hair – the Boy General.

The Kansans would be subjected to persistent harassment throughout their tribulation in the wilderness. The men from the "Show Me State" were driven by the need for revenge and determined to unite with the Custer element at the incipient Camp Supply.

When examined in full context, the expedition differed radically from the underequipped, undermanned, ineffectual patrols that been the mainstay of Army operations in the west.

At the direct order of President Andrew Johnson, these columns of iron men on gamboling, stamping war horses embodied a formidable killing machine organized along the lines of a full powered Union Civil War cavalry division. They sought combat, they sought the enemy, they hungered for contact as felon who long incarcerated, relishes his freedom to once more launch himself upon the unwary.

It was on the fifth freezing, sub-zero day, when moving downstream along the meandering, frozen Valley of the Beaver that they came upon the trail of a massive war party headed north.

Reflexively the Yellow Hair requested the cautious Lieutenant Colonel Sully his acquiescence to allow an attack on the Indian village from which the animal skin clad war party had originated.

The insightful Lieutenant Colonel Sully was laden with the burden of logistics, and for his own reasons remained conservative in his strategy. Thus, he denied his younger, more aggressive fellow officer the object of his passion.

To Sully's credit the column with its four hundred wagons achieved its objective on time; the enormous wheeled logistics train had reached the site of Camp Supply as scheduled. The dismounted cavalry were put to work like combat engineers constructing the fortification in the unseasonal winter wonderland.

It was unfortunate that Custer and Sully were diametrically opposite of one another. The tension that grew from their dissimilar personalities and leadership styles fomented dangerous resentment between the two men of equal rank.

The clash in their opinions of how the campaign was to be prosecuted would be realized at Camp Supply. The impetuous, mercurial Custer was by nature a risk taker and Sully was keen to stay within the carefully laid out plan; it was no mean task to maintain the cohesiveness of the lumbering, accident plagued 400 wagon train, with their drivers riding the left mule nearest the front wheel, guiding the mule at the front by means of a long reign. Close coordination was required between the driver and co-driver, who operated the brake. When the brake froze up, the wagon could not be stopped. Six mules pulled the massive wagons.

Aggressive by nature, the Yellow Hair champed at the bit and stamped at the hoof figuratively speaking, to have a go at the Indian village. His anger welled up in him like an enraged wolf leashed to a post and his pulse beat in his ears like the ear-splitting infantry drums of the Army of the Potomac. He cleared his throat and spat onto the crystalline snow.

"Coward!" recklessly accused the exasperated Lieutenant Colonel Custer.

The insult was totally unexpected by the forty-seven-year-old Lieutenant Colonel Sully, who felt the adrenaline shoot like an electrical charge into his gun hand. He felt the adrenaline in his wrist, hand and fingers. He sized up his younger opponent, aware that he was going to challenge an experienced killer to a duel. Sully couldn't have cared less! A man's honor was important, and if it meant getting killed over it, then the fight was worth it all. Sully was not a man to be underestimated, and the wrong man to insult.

Lieutenant Colonel Sully was a son of the prominent water colorist painter, Thomas Sully. Thomas Sully was widely popular and renowned for his painting of President John Quincy Adams, which was displayed in the National Gallery of Art, in Washington DC.

Lt Col Alfred Sully was an accomplished water colorist himself and also an Indian fighter of some repute. But having married a Sioux woman he was

40

held in disdain by nearly all of his fellow officers. Often, Sully was called a "squaw man" – albeit behind his back.

The detail-oriented Sully who preferred to execute the winter campaign in a careful portraiture of orchestrated brush strokes preferred to cut to the chase when it came to the "fast draw."

Custer, on the other hand could not afford to yield to his reflexive instinct. When his life depended on his speed to the hip leather, the Yellow Hair tried to be as meticulously prepared and forward thinking as he was capable of.

"Have at you, sir!" was the artist-warrior's verbal response, slapping Lieutenant Colonel Custer full across the left side of his face with his leather gauntlet, or riding glove.

"Gladly!" retorted the Yellow Hair, the air hissed between his straight, unstained teeth, always brushed and flossed.

"Since I am the one being challenged, I choose standard issue revolvers!" added Custer.

The Boy General studied the much older man standing before him. They both stood at average height, but Sully, West Point class of 1841 looked much the worse for wear.

Sully's low forehead, covered with a thick, oily mane of greying hair was concealed by the wide brimmed regulation blue felt slouch hat. His countenance was narrow, long and horse faced. Hazel irises glared at the Boy General from beneath heavy epicanthic folds. The corners of the eyes were downturned, conveying the impression of sadness to Sully's affect. But the artist's eyes glowed with the anticipation of a confident, seasoned killer.

"So be it, then!" replied Sully, adding, "Revolvers it shall be, tomorrow at sunup! Choose carefully your second!"

"My arse it will be sunup!" countered Custer, "Let it be now, I've not another moment to waste dallying with you!"

"There will be no dueling unless I have the honor to officiate!" interjected a baritone voice inflected with Irish brogue. General Sheridan swaggered simian like, bow legged to the outside of Custer's Sibley tent, where the two officers stood facing off each other.

Sheridan always ambulated in a deformed gait due to his short stature and tenure in the saddle, he stood his tallest at four feet eleven inches with his two-inch insoles placed in his cavalry boots.

Sully had served his purpose, reasoned Sheridan, biting off the corner a large plug of black, tarry chewing tobacco. Little Phil surmised that now Sully could be quickly gotten out of the way and the more aggressive Custer could run the show.

Not that Sheridan really favored the duel, but his escalating addiction to opium had involved Sully, and Sully's blurry connections to the smoke-filled dens of the Chinese underworld that was heavily involved in the construction of the Transcontinental Railway.

Sully was becoming a handful, wanting a promotion in exchange for supplying Sheridan's growing opioid dependence; he had tried to blackmail Little Phil. Things being as they were, figured General Sheridan, Sully needed to go.

"I'll have at this churlish girl of a man with your blessing, General Sheridan!" riposted Sully. His face was smooth shaven but for a moustache that extended from either side of his lips into a massive goatee shocked with gray. His jawline melded into a thick, ox-like neck which was partly obscured by the high collar of the frock coat he wore beneath the heavier buffalo skin coat.

"Clear an area forward and aft! Clear out a field of fire!" shouted Little Phil Sheridan.

"This dispute is about to be settled forthwith!" Sheridan's deep voice sounded as though it was spoken from the orifice of a large, heavy man, and coming as it did from a man of such short stature, never failed to surprise people.

Officers and NCOs shouted commands to the converging crowd of rowdy uniformed spectators. They formed up the men to either side of the contestants, careful to have the areas behind either shooter clear of onlookers.

Dark cumulonimbus clouds scudded overhead to the southeast as a norther cloaked the metallic, gunmetal gray sky. The situation was developing quickly, unexpectedly, and men hastily placed bets on the outcome. This duel would see fortunes made and lost.

Unnoticed to all but the Boy General, a cameraman struggled in the snow, setting up his large daguerreotype device. The camera was directed to capture the image of Sully. Custer frequently had a cameraman with him, recognizing the importance of photography to further his potential political career.

Sully stood ten paces from the Yellow Hair, both men had released the flap from their regulation holsters and folded them back into their pistol belts, leaving the handles of the Remington New Army revolvers exposed at the open top of the deep, black leather holsters.

"When I say draw, draw and start shooting!" shouted General Sheridan through cupped hands, so that all could hear him in the brutal arctic wind gusts.

In the scant amount of time Custer had in which to react before drawing his weapon, he shouted "Scholton! Are you ready?"

"No, General! Hold your horses a minute! I am setting up the camera!" responded Charles Scholten – the professional photographer under employ of the Boy General.

Thick set, and middle aged, Scholten's hair and beard were ungreyed. Scholten was often in the company of Custer in the field, and when not in the field as well.

On occasion, the photographer would be financially induced to shoot exquisite private portfolios of the wives of high ranking officers – those of the lower ranking officers, too – if they could swing the cash. The portfolios were often of a personal, private nature.

Scholten struggled in the snow as he readied the large, unwieldy camera apparatus. He remembered uneasily the last photo session he'd been coerced into shooting with the former general's wife, while the Yellow Hair was away. It had been at the request of the President of the United States, Elizabeth Custer had implied, without saying so directly.

The photos, of an explicit nature had been expedited in their transit to the White House through a former horseman for the defunct Pony Express, which had ceased operation in 1861.

These riders could still be had for a price and were the elite of the private couriers. Small and scrawny to aid the horses in their travel, their wallets were loaded with wads of cash. They were rich men, but it was a job fraught with risks.

No sooner had Scholton disappeared under the massive hood of the camera than Sheridan shouted, "Draw!"

Immediately Custer reached to his left side with his right hand, in an exquisite manifestation of the "crossdraw." Sully was going for his gun as Custer seemed to move in slow motion, crouching with knees bent and leaning forward as he took aim holding the Remington cap and ball .44 caliber revolver in both hands.

Sully had barely cleared his New Army revolver from its black regulation holster when he was suddenly and completely blinded by a huge flash from the photographer.

"Smile!" shouted Scholten as the powerful blast of light from the flare sized magnesium flash powder lamp exploded into brilliant incandescence.

The white flame of the magnesium flared several feet laterally and then soared to five feet above the Roman Candle-like torch. The torch burned brighter than the sun by many times. Scholten's eyes were tightly closed as he continued to hold the hand-held cartridge as high above his head as he could get it.

The artist turned gunfighter was completely blinded, shielding his eyes with his non-shooting hand.

The first bullet hit squarely in the center of Sully's forehead, making a loud smacking noise upon impact, like when a young lady slaps her lover viciously across the face.

The soft lead ball drilled through the thick frontal bone that protected Sully's brain at 800 feet per second, partially flattening as it did so. The resulting shock to the brain as the bullet dumped its kinetic energy into the fatty mass caused the gray matter to expand explosively and exit the nose and ears of Sully.

Custer didn't waste time; he moved quickly. The Boy General never took his focused eyes from the deadly threat which Sully still posed.

Skillfully, the Yellow Hair shifted his position through crafty foot work. Custer held his service revolver forward in his right hand as he violently struck the hammer spur with the heel of his left.

The remaining five bullets flew into his antagonist, who remained standing, frozen in place as if electrified. The liquefied mass in the man's skull no longer fit the definition of a brain, as such, and could not relay the message to the rest of the body that it was in fact dead.

Each bullet impact caused the nervous system of Sully's body to partially turn the standing cadaver from one side to the other, before collapsing as the knees gave out.

"A round of applause for Lieutenant Colonel Custer!" shouted General Sheridan. "Quartermaster! A shot of whiskey for all officers and two shots for enlisteds!"

"CUSTER! CUSTER! CUSTER!" shouted 800 cavalrymen along with the scouts who had seen the illegal duel transpire before their enlivened eyes.

Later, as Sully cooled his heels in a shallow grave, Sheridan spoke privately with the Boy General, who was still trying to unwind, and come down from the adrenal surge after his near-death experience.

Custer needed to sit down; he was dizzy, and discombobulated. He was in danger of hyperventilating and feared an asthma attack. He entered the Sibley tent followed by Sheridan and sat down heavily on a field chair. Custer was leaning his head back and subduing his rapid breathing into controlled, measured breaths.

"You're short about a thousand men," Little Phil reminded Custer, "are you certain you wish to proceed less the Kansans?"

"Yes," replied the Boy General, "there is no time to waste. Never mind the Indian village that caused the dispute between Sully and myself; now that I'm in command – I have bigger fish to fry," replied Custer, catching his breath and fighting down the wave of clammy nausea.

"And it stands to reason, as well," agreed Sheridan, "Governor Crawford will certainly pull rank on you and seek to control the campaign. The politics of orchestrating this is akin to coordinating puppets by means of strings. I have endeavored from the moment of this plan's inception to have you lead it."

Sheridan spoke in irony, for in fact, it was the despot in Washington DC who had through General Grant, ordered Sherman choose Custer to lead the assault column.

"Let me tell you something else, George Armstrong Custer. I'm an opium addict. You know that. An opium addict will go loco if he can't sustain his dependence – if he can't get the good stuff – the real thing," said

Sheridan, pausing for a moment before continuing, "you're an addict, too. But you're addicted to killing – just look at you. You can't say that you're not. The relief that you are feeling right now as you come down off of that adrenal rush is indescribable."

Chapter Five: The Women

Hundreds of miles away from where General Sheridan discussed the inner demons of himself with those of his junior officer, Libby Custer had her own concerns; these were centered around hunger.

"Land of Goshen! By the good Heavens, that supper that Eliza is preparing imparts a most sumptuous and delectable aroma!" Elizabeth Bacon Custer, the eloquent wife of the controversial former general exclaimed effervescently.

"Come on in here all you hungry young white ladies!" called an earthy, convivial female African American voice from the large dining room.

The dining room was in one of the block houses of quarried granite which served as an officer's quarters. Elizabeth Custer often followed her husband about on his adventures – even when it meant going into the field and living in her husband's Sibley tent.

She kept a diary and wrote books based on their adventures. But not this time; this time she was in a different temporary home - one of the luxurious base housing units at Fort Dodge, Kansas.

Elizabeth deigned to stay in this home of mortar and granite. This was a strong house, hewn and blasted from the grips of the land. The stone had been wrenched as though from the grudgingly yielding clutches of Gaia, mother of the earth.

Gaia was the Titan that lived within the quarries, where men died. Where men died blown to pieces with dynamite, where men died crushed beneath falling rock, and where men died locked in deadly embrace with their mortal enemy – the Cheyenne.

Within these walls of quarried stone was a conclave, an entourage that shielded Elizabeth – the paradigm of beauty from loneliness; this consisted of her sister in law Margaret, close friend Beverly Sumrall, and the true matron of the house – Eliza.

The home was built like a fortified blockhouse, and it needed to be. While the lavish officer's quarters would have been the most important consideration for most officers' wives, this was not so with Elizabeth Custer. Beautiful, yet sanguinary, she was the daughter of the respected hanging judge of Monroe, Michigan - Judge Daniel Stanton Bacon. Elizabeth Bacon Custer immediately was impressed by the grim, stalwart defensive nature inherent of the structure's design.

The venerated Judge Bacon's daughter had spent the majority of her early years in a series of all female parochial schools, through which she developed an affinity toward the company of her peers.

Sometimes months would pass, several years at times, without Libbie seeing a male while matriculating within these insulated institutions of higher learning. She grew from prepubescence into adulthood within a cloistered, monastic world absent of men.

The strict curriculum included lessons in advanced Latin and Greek, taught by austere, intellectually gifted spinster school teachers who did not elaborate as to why they wore no wedding band.

The situation being as it was, there were no occasions - no windows of opportunity that enabled the development of disruptive, immature fixations on the opposite sex; they did not exist in her world. Situations which fomented envies did exist, however, in this Lesbos-like island of academia.

It was the setting itself, that nurtured the odd, muliebrous personalities that had in their competitive focus, female upper classmates; women who were rapidly maturing in more than their intellectual repertoire. In this world destitute of men, the impressionable Elizabeth aspired to emulate the gynecocentric attributes of her upper-classmates.

Had Elizabeth's formative years transpired within a more conventional setting, she may have reflected the attributes of a Tom Boy. As it was, she sought respite from the demanding academic curriculum through gymnasium – and those minutes in the changing room with her upper-class mates, whose maturing forms she envied.

The graduating classes of every academic year included eighteen and nineteen-year-old women who had never seen a man in the truest sense; shoved out of the way almost in infancy by unloving parents who preferred childless wedlock, free of the encumbrances of parenthood. These women had not a clue what a man was, although they were privy to rumor and speculation.

These students were prized by the faculty and groomed for a career in higher learning. Libbie fell into a notch just barely above that of the shut-in students, who were abandoned by family and shoved off into a maternal institution that was almost a nunnery.

Elizabeth Bacon considered Hellenistic beauty to be the penultimate esthetic attainment possible for a woman. She determined to emulate her upper classwomen in the years to come, when her time came to exhibit her maturity in the openness of gymnasium.

Now, relegated to the status of wife to a living legend, Elizabeth Bacon Custer longed for those cherished, halcyon days of yesteryear. Infrequently she enjoyed the opportunity to be the Goya model. Libbie could be the nonchalant nude, feigning unawareness that there was anything extraordinary as she let fall her petticoats.

The audience, in a manner of speaking, would continue talking about some mundane topic as though it could obfuscate her opportune burlesque performance. She felt their eyes on her. Be it officer's wives, female servants, or women kinfolk, it was all an opportunity for the thespian.

"I betch y'all po' white Ladies is jus' starvin' Marvins'! Well this be a good, rib stickin' meal what strap some sow belly on yall's po' empty, heavin' tummies!" continued Eliza, the Custer's maid servant, majordomo, and concierge.

"Mmmmmm, mmmmmm, mmmmmmmph!" Eliza added huskily for emphasis, her hands on her thin, muscular hips.

Despite the sumptuous feasts that the energetic woman prepared three times a day, she remained whip thin. The muscles that played like oiled rope beneath the loose dress were slave muscles, developed to their fullest potential on the plantation fields of Virginia.

Eliza had been a childhood playmate of the daughters of the plantation owner. The spoiled scions persuaded the worldly tobacco tycoon to employ Eliza as a house slave. Eliza was thus brought indoors and instructed in the culinary arts of the great kitchen.

And she came to know the peculiar ways of the strange white women within the high-ceilinged walls of that great house, in antebellum Virginia. Then, the master's sons had all been conscripted and force fed into the rifle companies of Lee's Army of Northern Virginia – to be killed in action almost immediately.

It was then that Eliza had fled – fled toward the sound of distant cannon fire that carried through the Valley of the Shenandoah like the thunder of some distant, growing storm.

It was no mean feat to low crawl on her belly, through the Confederate lines without being detected. No mean feat either, to make it to the Union lines without being shot to pieces.

It was there, standing outside a Sibley tent that Eliza saw the Boy General for the first time.

"Look!" said a Union private, who was escorting the emancipated former slave through the camp toward one of the dozens of mess tents for breakfast.

"There stands the Boy General! General George Armstrong Custer! The youngest general in the history of the Army! There he stands with his comely wife, Elizabeth! Elizabeth Bacon Custer!" exclaimed the private, the tone of his voice was embellished in pride – to be able to personally see and point out the personage of the Boy General to Eliza.

"Why, I've never before seen such a mo' beautiful picture in all of my life!" exclaimed Eliza, taking leave of the private, after asking him to fetch the accoutrements to prepare a feast for the young couple that had riveted her attention.

"My lands!" exclaimed the Negress as she approached the affable and receptive Custers. "Yall jus' starvin'! Lemme get the stove in yall's tent a goin' with some fresh, pipin' hot coffee lak only Eliza knows how to brew! Then I get some breakfast a cookin' an' flesh out yall's lean hips!"

From that day in 1864 and ever since, Eliza had ministered to the Custers' every need.

Eliza wore a plain cotton green striped work dress in which the sleeves were not too long and bottom of the skirt not overlarge in circumference as she bustled about, ensuring all was properly set at the massive wooden table.

The heavy supper table was made of lustrous pecan wood, stained and rubbed with linseed oil, bringing out the deep natural beauty of the dark wood grain and at the same time filling in the scratches and gouges that it had sustained in its remarkable voyage from the east coast.

On either side of the fine porcelain chinaware were silver spoons, forks, and knives ensconced within carefully folded napkins. A baroque, oversized epergne made of blue tinted cut glass had been placed in the center of the extended table.

The epergne was filled with white magnolia blossoms, preserved in an ice filled storm cellar – the honey sweet scent was discernable even among the

56

smells of the meal that overwhelmed the dining room and permeated throughout the home. Once complete, the table setting made for a sumptuous display of esculent ecstasy.

The enticing aroma of pheasant soup wafted from a polished sterling tureen.

Roasted buffalo loin teasingly spiced with minced almond, garlic and coarse chopped chicory graced the center of a large sterling silver platter. The loin had been basted in a ruddy Bordeaux wine and was fringed with wafer thin slices of succulent buffalo tongue.

Yellow slabs of steaming hot cornbread and black-eyed peas in porcelain bowls adorned with intricate designs helped to embellish the delectable array. Pecan pie and pound cake that had been flavored with finely ground tobacco snuff hinted at a delectable "bonne bouche" of desserts to follow the main entrée.

Bottles of fine champagne chilled in buckets of ice, procured during the winter storm. Normally, ice from the previous winter would be stored in storm cellars and preserved, packed in sawdust.

Storm cellars were a must in this land, where tornados ripped through with no warning. Even the smallest clapboard houses on the most barren, destitute, worn out farmsteads had them.

Although Elizabeth and George Armstrong Custer were both teetotalers, Libbie Custer seldom refrained from providing all available forms of alcohol to her guests – in particular her female guests.

Libbie and George Armstrong were fond of drinking strong, bitter coffee instead, from a massive urn made of pewter.

The ladies quickly sat themselves to the task of devouring the banquet that Eliza had set before them, and as they ate, fell to talking of the gossip pertaining to the other officers and their wives, and of the Grim Family Circus that was overdue to arrive in town.

The horrific early onset of winter had delayed the circus by a number of days. The Grim Family Circus was not famous, per se, but was made known primarily through the numerous deaths that seemed to follow it, like vultures following an army.

"Won't you have some more champagne, Beverly?" offered Margaret, who was quite tipsy.

Elizabeth observed the drunken discourse of her sister in law discreetly from beneath eyelashes lined with mascara. She savored the spiced, greasy slice of buffalo tongue that almost melted in her mouth as she watched her sister in law's almost indiscreet obsession with Beverly.

The dining table chair squeaked as it slid against the grain of the polished oak floor as Elizabeth stood up. Libbie politely excused herself, exhibiting the etiquette instilled upon her at the boarding schools. "Eliza, that was yet another decisive culinary triumph

58

in the war against hunger - the most delectable meal of which I have ever had the pleasure to ingest!" complimented Libbie, adding almost as an afterthought, "Why! I practically ingurgitated the entire panoply of comestibles!"

"Oh Libbie!" exclaimed Margaret Custer, "I never tire hearing you speak those words of yours!" exclaimed the former general's sister as she also stood, making a conscious effort to maintain her balance. The room seemed to spin as she tried to hide her champagne induced inebriation. Margaret complimented Eliza tipsily, "I have to amplify what Libbie said, Eliza! You truly outdid yourself on this one!"

Margaret's features were attractive in a handsome sort of way, and her cheeks were flushed with the alcohol. Dark blond – almost red hair was piled loosely above a forehead which gently sloped back; it was not a high forehead. The pronounced occipital ridge emphasized, rather than detracted from the large brown eyes that continually made contact with those of Beverly. However, it was the occipital ridge that kept her from being pretty and yet added to her beauty in the masculine sense. The outstanding feature of her face was a finely shaped, petite nose, upturned at the tip. The full mouth, with pouting lips was downturned at the corners and underslung with a well-formed chin set onto a firm jaw. Her athletic neck was hidden by the high collar of her dinner dress.

"I beg forgiveness, but I deign remain seated at this epic banquet that Eliza has prepared. I fear I am to be gluttonous this night!" apologized Beverly Sumrall, as she forced herself to laugh politely, eyeing the two sisters in law as they left the dining room and entered the bedroom of Libbie. "What a strange pair those two make," she thought to herself.

Chapter Six: The Advance to Contact

The aromas wafting provocatively from a set table were far from the mind of the Yellow Hair as he pulled his wool scarf more tightly against his face, made raw and chapped in the freezing wind.

Bitter, bone cracking cold had set a freezing death-grip on the plains by the twenty-third of November. The Seventh Cavalry, dressed in heavy winter clothing departed in column from Camp Supply in an artic type blizzard during white out conditions. White out conditions were winter phenomena in which total whiteness prevailed within the visual spectrum of the human eye.

Never to be found in the rear, the Boy General again led the column personally; he guided the force of 800 cavalry including their attachments in the blinding whiteness that epitomized the scale, and the fury of the blizzard.

He used his four-ounce, inch and a half in diameter magnetic pocket compass.

The navigational compass, popular among officers during the recent Civil War was enclosed within a brass case that had the outward appearance of a pocket watch. What set this compass apart was that it was one of the few available Ritchies.

Ritchies were advanced, state of the art and liquid filled. The Ritchie was a hand held marine compass with a floating indicator; the precursor of all modern magnetic compasses.

The Boy General reveled in outdoorsmanship. He was, in fact, widely read and his scope of knowledge in field craft was expansive.

Additionally, he was an amateur geologist, scientist, taxidermist and actor. In another time he would have certainly been a Renaissance Man.

The multi-talented commanding officer was also a gifted writer with an avid readership which he cultivated for the future, when his designs for political office would come to the fore.

When it came to the outdoors however, it was as though there were a Davy Crockett somewhere in his convoluted mind. In the skill of land navigation using map and compass there were few his equal.

Often, he would set up a complicated land navigation course and have his officers compete in it, using their more rudimentary, hand me down compasses so prevalent in the Army following the recent Civil War.

The elongated main column halted and set up camp in order to allow the heavily escorted train of forty supply wagons to catch up. Seven of which were loaded down with critical ammunition. In addition to ammunition, the wagons carried limited supplies and forage for the horses.

The balance of 360 wagons remained at Camp Supply, where the tardy elements of Crawford and the others were only now arriving.

Everything had to be ready before cautiously crossing the swollen, ice choked Canadian River. The Canadian was the largest tributary which fed the Arkansas River. It was some 900 miles in length, originating from the Sangre de Cristo Mountains in New Mexico, extending inexorably through the dry wastes of the Texas Panhandle and into the Oklahoma Indian Territory.

The command had been stretched out over a length of four tortuous miles, in part owing to wagons which occasionally slid on the ice and slipped off the path – sometimes smashing their wheels, crippling their mules, and worse – killing the teamster that directed the wagon while mounted on one of the six mules.

During the lull before the crossing, the controversial twenty-eight-year-old Major Elliott had been sent out on reconnaissance. Elliott had been the defacto commanding officer of the Seventh Cavalry during Custer's one-year hiatus following his court martial.

The court martial held at Fort Leavenworth, Kansas concluded on October 11, 1867. Custer had been found guilty of five of the eleven charges brought against him. Lieutenant Colonel Custer had been suspended from rank and command for one year, with total forfeiture of pay. The court martial was lengthy and fraught with complicated turns and twists. But to encapsulate it in an oversimplification, Custer got into bad trouble when he issued shoot to kill orders on deserters.

The conclusion of the court martial had delighted General Ulysses S. Grant, but General Sherman's reaction had been tepid and noncommittal. However, it was General Sheridan who would provide his own personal lodgings to Custer and his wife. General Sheridan was singular in that he seemed the only one of Custer's colleagues to show any real degree of honor and decency toward his friend following the humiliating verdict.

Elliott's reconnaissance mission was extremely important and fraught with risk. The task was barely completed when Scout Jack Corbin, armed with two revolvers and a Sharps carbine was sighted struggling through the snow with an urgent message – it was from Elliott. Corbin's normally dark beard was white with frozen condensation from his breath.

Corbin relayed to Custer that Elliott had located a Cheyenne village of moderate size and was on his way back to give the commanding officer an up to date situation report. He would also contribute to construction of an accurate model of the village to be laid out on the floor of Custer's Sibley tent.

The supply wagons had not yet all arrived at the camp when Custer received Major Elliott within his coveted tent. Custer was fond of conducting officers' meetings within his adored tent. The two officers discussed the details of Elliott's reconnaissance while Custer prepared for the staff meeting within the tepee shaped canvas dome.

Inside the confines of the crowded interior of the twelve feet high, eighteen feet in diameter Sibley tent was an oasis of warmth. The convivial atmosphere within the Sibley juxtaposed starkly against the howling blizzard that had begun to rage outside yet again. The scouts and officers had removed their caps made of badger fur and their warm rabbit fur lined mittens. Within the Sibley, which Custer took everywhere with him – it didn't matter where, a bed of coals rested glowing. The amber coals lay within the conical, sheet iron Sibley stove. The telescoping tent pole that erected the tepee shaped canvas tent was supported by a metal tripod. The Sibley stove nestled against the tripod and the smoke was vectored up the stovepipe and out the top of the tent, which was open topped, like a tepee.

The effectiveness of the Sibley stove in warming the tepee shaped tent did not go unappreciated by the personnel whose attention was directed to the blond-haired officer who addressed them.

While the majority of the soldierly host was miserable in the inclement weather of the outdoors, this was not the case with the Yellow Hair; Custer was an avid outdoorsman who loved camping – and could set up his Sibley tent unassisted in under seven minutes. He would even refuse assistance while immersed in the setting up of the Sibley. He would lose himself in it, the responsibilities of command were for the seven minutes it took for Custer to erect the tent – gone.

Secretly, Custer was observing to see if any of his staff paid attention to his nice tent, with its matching stove – both of which were the top of the line Sibleys. When it came to camping, the outdoors enthusiast spared no expenses on his passion. He took note of who paid compliments to his nice camping equipment – and who didn't…

Custer spoke to the gathered group of officers within the Sibley tent; all were taking notes as he issued a rash of abbreviated, fragmented orders known as "frags." These frags had originated from a lengthy operations order Custer had prepared before he left for the field, known as a "five paragraph order."

During the explanation of the frags, Custer was spelling out what each officer was entailed to do, waiting until almost the last to address twenty-four-year-old Captain Louis M. Hamilton – at the time, the youngest captain in the Regular Army.

Hamilton had earned his rank the hard way; drawing first blood as a second lieutenant in the Third US Infantry Division as a company commander during the horrific Union repulse at Fredericksburg, Virginia.

Hamilton won brevets at Chancellorsville and Gettysburg and made first lieutenant in May 1864. He was also the grandson of Alexander Hamilton – a fact that had caused Custer to personally draw up the duty roster, assuring that Hamilton would not be in the lead element.

The entrance to the Sibley was a flap of burlap material, and it was tied closed to retain the heat radiated from the Sibley stove. The daylight that penetrated weakly through the canvas walls of the tent was augmented by sputtering whale oil lanterns. These cast a dim, wavering illumination over the sandbox like terrain features that lay to the front of the stove. About the diorama kneeled the scouts, behind them stood the officers.

Custer had a pointer stick which he was using to effectively point out the terrain features set within the diorama before the officers and scouts. The ridgelines, hills, and valleys along with the Washita River were skillfully replicated in miniature, even down to the tiny tepees that composed the moderate Cheyenne Indian encampment.

"I am dividing the 800-man attack force into four distinct assault elements, with the purpose of surrounding the village prior to the assault at dawn," the Lieutenant Colonel's voice proclaimed his intent in a concise set of staccato bursts, emphasized by the flash of flossed, brushed teeth from the mustached mouth. The words were hoarse, owing to Custer's strep throat and bad cold.

"Major Elliott," rasped Custer, "you are to take group one and circle east. Captain William Thompson, you are to take group two and circle west. If you have no questions, make final arrangements and move out."

The two elements detached quickly, and after only thirty minutes set out on their mission. The lieutenant colonel then completed his instructions to the remaining two groups. Shortly thereafter, the third group would move to the nearby timber stand to the west and be firmly established long before dawn. Custer would take the fourth group along with the Osages, scouts and sharpshooters and then prepare to attack frontally.

The influential governor of Kansas, Samuel J. Crawford had vehemently insisted on the inclusion of the Osage scouts. It was more than their keen knowledge of the Oklahoma Indian Territory that Crawford coveted - it was their blood feud with the Cheyenne. The state of war that characterized the acrimonious relations between the Osage and the Cheyenne reached back into the distant past, vanishing into the swirling mists of time...

Lt James Bell was in charge of the seven ammunition wagons and was instructed to make for the village at the commencement of firing. However, Bell's ammunition wagons would be left further back during the final approach so as not to make noise and arouse the sleeping village.

The former general intended to employ Sheridan's plan of a double envelopment against Black Kettle's modest village of fifty-one tepees. A double envelopment was no mean feat and required skill and luck – everything had to go correctly in order for a double envelopment to succeed.

Moments earlier, while yet in the Sibley tent prior to the departure of the groups under Elliott and Thompson, Custer had asked at the end of the five-paragraph order, "Are there any questions?"

"Yes Sir," offered the short, pudgy Hamilton. "Might I ask to lead my troops?"

"Hamilton, you're the Officer of the Day and you'll remain behind with the main body of the wagon train. The wagon train is to be left behind along with eighty men to accompany it. You'll follow as best you can, it's an important job," explained Custer as he reiterated the administrations and logistics of the frag, "seven ammunition wagons will detach from you, led by Lieutenant Bell and link with the assault element when the attack begins," Custer spoke fast, often restarting his sentences before completing them. He was prone to stammer when under stress. And under stress he was, when it came to Hamilton.

"Surely, sir, there must be some way…" pleaded the grandson of Alexander Hamilton, one of the nation's Founding Fathers and architect of the US Treasury Department.

"Look at it from my point of view now, Captain Hamilton, you're the Officer of the Day and we can't be jostling the schedule about. Wouldn't be fair to the other officers," riposted Custer adroitly, his response had been prepared ahead of time in anticipation of the request.

The Yellow Hair added "Some of the group commanders are already on their way. Now, may I entertain any further questions, Captain?"

"Yes sir," replied Hamilton yet once more, "Might I have a word in frank dialogue with the Lieutenant Colonel regarding the duty roster?"

Now came the part that Custer had been dreading. He knew that Captain Hamilton was determined to lead his company in the attack. The Boy General was trying to do everything within his command authority to keep this valuable asset from being harmed.

Lieutenant Colonel Custer dismissed his remaining cadre and faced Hamilton "Yes, Captain, but the duty roster is set, and the assault elements are moving into their attack positions. Now is not the time for changes to the duty roster; it's too late."

"There is a lieutenant who is snow blind, he has accepted the offer I made to trade my position for his," riposted Hamilton. Lieutenant Colonel Custer felt his blood congeal as he realized he was outmaneuvered and forced to accede to the request of his captain.

Custer remembered uneasily the threat implied by his two commanding officers; "Lose that boy," Sherman had warned, "Lose that boy," Sheridan had echoed, "and you will not see general again."

70

Chapter Seven: Enter, President Johnson

Far to the east, at the White House, the success or failure of Custer's mission worried the Commander in Chief. President Johnson's office was located in the central part of the structure and faced the Potomac River.

The room from which Johnson directed the course of the country was as drab as the furniture was worn.

A heavy armchair which had seen better days waited in front of unwashed windows for some brave soul to sit upon it. There was a worn-out bureau made of mahogany along with a smaller desk sort of pushed out of the way beside a wall. Atop them were maps of the Oklahoma Indian Territory and Kansas.

It was the large, expansive table made of lustrous black walnut, centered like a focal point in the big room which Johnson used for his tedious work. A duo of leather settees stuffed with horsehair were measured off equidistantly from the desk.

A massive painting of President Andrew Johnson glared hatefully from the wall, over the huge fireplace.

Another, even more sinister appearing portraiture of Johnson as a younger man hung sneering malevolently from the same wall several feet from the fireplace.

Whale oil lanterns often supplemented the less dependable and sometimes dangerous gas lights.

The president stood in front of the windows that faced outward toward the Potomac River. Then, contemplating the possibility that a sniper could get a shot at him, he pulled the heavy purple curtains closed.

The unpredictable, schizophrenic President Johnson found himself under heavy pressure to put a halt to the murderous Indian depredations. The imperious demands of the desperate governors of the ravaged, devastated states had provoked the paranoid, ruthless president into murderous action.

The strapping, muscular seventeenth President of the United States stood at five feet ten inches in height but seemed larger as he turned once more to face his head of security.

The unpredictable POTUS regarded the man who sat confidently before him with one leg crossed over the other. This man was of a similar build to the president but was barrel chested and his heavy gut was held in by a corset type vest.

"My sources tell me that recently Sheridan had ridden out to meet with Custer," stated the seated man, his small mouth was set in a jowl face and he chose his words carefully.

President Johnson was a distrustful, suspicious man who trusted no one. He suspected everyone, and he suspected that the man who sat before him was yet another one of the sycophantic men he dares not rely on.

"I last spoke with Sheridan a month ago, Allen. I had trusted him and took him at his word. I had assumed that he would be returning to Washington by now to give me an update on the situation developing in the Oklahoma Indian Territory. He was not forthright with me, and I am of the opinion that he would connive to see Custer tarry in his campaign," responded President Andrew Johnson.

"If Custer is directed by Sheridan not to attack," continued Johnson to Allen Pinkerton, "then I may very well face impeachment proceedings. The governors of the outlying regions are claiming that I can do nothing to protect them from the Indians. I know that there are people in the military, in the government – people everywhere who want to see me fail. They are out to do me no good."

The president paused in his monologue, and then continued, "Sheridan is out to get me, along with Grant. They both are. There are probably more, too. There's just no way of telling."

"Mr. President, it's true that Sheridan had gone to see Custer. But as to Generals Sheridan and Grant being complicit in a conspiracy to see you impeached – that is sheer speculation. I have received no intelligence to support that assumption. Sheridan means to see that Custer has all that he needs. But to attempt to undermine the President of the United States," replied Pinkerton, Johnson's head of security, "well that's just not born out by the facts."

"I can't even trust you, Pinkerton. Here you are, defending those conspirators," retorted the president.

Johnson felt his pulse gallop with the rage that was beginning to well up within his breast.

"You're in league with them, aren't you?" accused the despotic commander in chief. His rummy, suspicious eyes beamed into the Scotsman from behind eyelids narrowed into slits of distrust.

Pinkerton nervously shifted in his chair, he felt a cold, clammy sweat bead on his forehead and his palms itched.

"YOU SON OF A BITCH!!!" shouted the president, his face was contorted grotesquely in a visage of scarlet rage.

President Johnson quickly closed the distance and brusquely grabbed Pinkerton from the chair. The president slammed the big man against the very desk that had been used by President Lincoln.

Pinkerton flew into the desk with such force that stacks of official documents that needed to be signed and tomes of important stationary flew in all directions from the cluttered top.

"Mr. President!" shouted Allen Pinkerton. "Grant did tell me that he didn't like you!" Pinkerton lied, knowing that it might save his life.

President Johnson was a feared man, known for his explosive outbursts of temper. He lifted Pinkerton above his head and threw him to the floor.

Then the president turned about and leaned forward, clenching the edge of Lincoln's desk. He clutched the desk with such force that the tendons stood out on the back of his powerful hands.

Andrew Johnson's face had reddened, and the veins distended on his temples. Drool dripped from the sneering, malignant mouth as the facial muscles quivered in a paroxysm of barely controlled rage.

Johnson's forehead above his deeply lined brow was expansive. The top of the head was crowned with disheveled graying hair that receded abruptly at the temples, presenting a conspicuous tongue of hair that stubbornly remained in the center.

Untrimmed, sooty, ludicrous eyebrows furrowed evilly above the menacing, distrusting, obsidian eyes.

President Johnson's narrow upper lip was rendered inconspicuous by the robust, sulking lower lip. The glowering mouth was etched in frown lines. The orifice appeared more malevolent owing to the overhung, downward turning, hook-like bird of prey nose. Decades devoted to the heavy drinking of hard liquor had cauliflowered the ugly nose.

The POTUS constantly suffered from kidney stones and migraines from his out of control hypertension. The seventeenth president regularly reacted violently to those who annoyed him and to those he did not trust.

"I heard him say it," continued Allen Pinkerton, "he doesn't like you."

Pinkerton was picking himself up from the floor and wiping the blood from his lip. Johnson's chief of security lived in constant fear for his life when he was alone with the president.

Pinkerton waited nervously for the president's fit of anger to pass. The White House Security man watched the square jaw of the despot pronounce itself as the muscles grew taught. Droplets of sweat flew from Johnson's mop of hair as he reeled back in sudden pain. The cleft of his chin became at once pronounced as he cursed.

"Damn it to hell!" shouted the president, reaching behind his lower back with both hands and massaging his ravaged kidneys.

"Gonna piss blood tonight!" growled Johnson as he bent backwards in an effort to rub his kidneys harder. Pinkerton saw Johnson reach for the handle of the Model 1858 Remington New Army revolver he always carried and remove it from the expensive shoulder rig he wore over his vest.

"Mr. President, I've already put a man on General Grant," lied the chief of the president's security.

Pinkerton had to think fast – his life depended on it.

"Anybody who says that they don't like you can't be trusted, especially the nation's highest ranking general," reiterated the big Scotsman.

President Johnson removed the revolver from the tanned, hand tooled, shining leather shoulder holster. Johnson liked the way the shoulder rig complimented his Baxter black suede vest. The president liked to carry concealed, and never went anywhere unarmed despite the massive security personnel that was always at hand.

The man in the White House was bi-polar and schizophrenic. The president was at no time ever certain of the loyalty of the people Pinkerton assigned to protect him. It was for this reason that he had a retinue of Negro Medal of Honor recipients to augment his personal security.

"Good idea, Allen," answered the president, setting the revolver on the desk temporarily to afford him flexibility as he continued massaging his back, "I don't trust Grant. Never have."

The unpredictable Johnson had on a long-sleeved button-down shirt, perfectly tailored with an open neck and turn over collar. His black, austere cravat was wide and not tight. The cravat was tied in a loop and held in place with a gold stickpin.

Much was speculated about the president. Johnson was known to design and sew his own clothing. He would tailor his clothing to accentuate his powerful build so that he could intimidate others.

Curiously, the hated president could have been the subject of a Horatio Algiers success story; of a boy born poor but made good - a prototypical rags to riches story.

Andrew Johnson had been born very poor. He was said to be illegitimate; a child born of affairs that his widowed wash-woman mother performed to supplement her meager income.

The preadolescent Andrew had been indentured to a renown tailor, and he liked the work so much that he became good at it. Good enough to skip out on his indentured contract in South Carolina at fifteen years of age and flee to Tennessee where he started his own tailor business.

What led to his unlikely role as president was nothing but a series of chances.

He had become a wealthy slave holding plantation owner and then the governor of Tennessee. Although pro-slavery, Johnson was anti-secession, and his unpopular decision to side with the North when the Civil War began led to his ouster from office.

Johnson had the Devil's Luck and during the Civil War he had doggedly stuck with the North. Then, as luck would have it, Johnson was at the right place at the right time yet again, and Lincoln chose him as his running mate against General McClellan in 1864.

McClellan's campaign was run on the platform of a negotiated settlement with the South, and Lincoln's platform was that of the unconditional surrender of the Confederacy.

Lincoln had picked Johnson based on practicality; Johnson owned slaves and President Lincoln shrewdly attempted to divide the Confederacy by drawing slave owners to his cause. It was a sort of marriage of convenience between the dissimilar personalities of Lincoln and Johnson.

Then after Lincoln had won, he was assassinated. As luck would have it - Johnson was thrust onto the most powerful position on earth.

Johnson was akin to a Shakespeare's *Dwarf in Giant's Clothes*; the paranoid schizophrenic would now strut his moment upon the world's stage, but his corrosive personality, confrontational bullying, and inability to compromise were traits that quickly netted him countless dangerous and powerful enemies.

Johnson would in time become known as "the most hated president in United States history."

If that were not enough, Johnson had a long history of brain splitting migraines that would sometimes incapacitate him. Later, medical authorities would attribute the headaches to a developing cerebral aneurism.

Always, too, a prodding, almost paralyzing agony in his lower back related to kidney stones plagued the Saul-like despot.

"It all comes as no surprise to me! I've suspected it all along! And I now have it on the good word from you, Allen Pinkerton," the president replied acidly to chief of White House security.

The president walked quickly across the room despite his pain, checking behind the curtains of one of the massive windows to assure that no assassins were present.

"And that's not all Allen," Johnson added, as he resumed rubbing the small of his back.

President Johnson regarded Allen Pinkerton critically. There was something he didn't like about the man, and something he did like about him at the same time.

That Pinkerton had let Lincoln down at Ford's theater was always at the forefront of Johnson's troubled mind.

"And that's not all - I don't put too much stock into what you have to say, Pinkerton," stated President Johnson.

"Your information was given to hyperbole and most of the time proved equivocal during the rebellion.

You didn't provide such hot-shit security for Lincoln, either," the president added crassly.

"But Mr. President," interrupted Pinkerton skillfully, seizing advantage of the president's paranoia to distract him from the direction that President Johnson was guiding the conversation.

"Grant doesn't like Custer either, and didn't you say that Custer was one of the only heroes of the war that you could truly trust?" interpolated Pinkerton.

President Johnson sat down heavily on Lincoln's leather-bound swivel chair behind the massive desk. He leaned back, placing his hands behind his bull neck and laced his fingers together.

Johnson studied the sweating man standing bravely before him. Maybe it was that, thought Johnson. Maybe the fact that Pinkerton had guts, maybe that's what he liked about him.

"Yeah. You've got a point there, alright, Pinkerton," conceded the president, adding, "Grant had the Boy General fucking court martialed over shooting those damned deserters! Then the cur had the audacity to laugh at him! He laughed at one of the only friends I have! He tried to ruin my friend and he laughed!"

"Certainly," Johnson admitted, "it had crossed my mind before now, that Grant could have it in for Custer as well as myself. Only a fool would not consider the possibility. But Grant is a shrewd one. He never once placed himself at the head of his troops during battle – like at Shiloh, always compelling his subordinates to do the risky work for him.

"Look at Cold Harbor! 7,000 brave Union soldiers killed in ten minutes – while Grant was safely in his tent looking over the map! So, it stands to reason that he has sent an assassin to murder me while he stands aloft in the background; something he's so good at! Also, he clearly intends for Custer to be killed in the high-risk campaign into the Washita!"

"I want to let you in on a little secret," said the White House security man, making up his mind and using his most powerful trump card in a bid to add credence to the growing list of false accusations against General Grant, and preserve his own life.

"Everyone is hiding secrets from me," answered the POTUS, "you are too, and you had better lay them out on the table for me."

"Not me," assured Pinkerton. "It's Grant. He's been intercepting the correspondence between you and Elizabeth Custer."

"How could you possibly know that?!!! Imbecile! Fool!!!" reacted the president, his face beginning to redden once more.

"It's my job to know, Mr. President!" responded Allen Pinkerton, standing up to the bully and putting his life on the line.

"I have this envelope, taken from beneath the bed mattress of General Grant," added Pinkerton.

The seal of the large manila envelope was not unbroken, and within it was a thick portfolio of daguerreotypes of a vivacious female of classical beauty. The portfolio was a nude study of exquisite design.

"Grant has the audacity to intercept my mail and keep it beneath his bed mattress like a pervert," mumbled Johnson to himself.

The deep lines of the president's forehead were furrowed in concentration as he studied the female images on the daguerreotypes through narrowed pig-like eyes.

"No small wonder then, that I haven't been receiving the mail! That was part of the deal; I give the Boy General a shot at command of the expedition in return for pics of her," exclaimed the president to Pinkerton, who was unsure if the words came in the form of a statement of fact or an admission guilt. Maybe it was both, Allen Pinkerton thought.

President Johnson pulled open the top center drawer of the massive desk and placed the daguerreotypes into a thick stack of similar photos of the same woman.

"Custer doesn't know to what lengths his wife will go to see him get promoted," confided the president.

Pinkerton did not reply, because he was stunned and speechless at the import of the president's open-ended statement – at what it implied.

The president would be even more stunned to learn, that it was he, Allen Pinkerton, who had been intercepting the mail correspondence between Elizabeth Custer and the despot.

"What kind of sick mind would compel a man to do such a thing, Mr. President?" asked Pinkerton, his growing relief was evidenced in his voice and Johnston did not notice as he stewed over what to do with his troublesome commanding general.

"No way I can shit-can him. The Army would be up in arms against me," admitted Johnson, "but there is another way," he smiled.

Allen Pinkerton felt the hairs on the back of his furry arms stand up in horror as he speculated on the sick mechanization that characterized President Johnson's aberrant personality.

"What other way?" asked Pinkerton.

"Come on!" answered the president, the tone of his voice conveyed an affable and effervescent mood as he added, "I'll show you! Let's descend into the basement! Sometimes I like to work off a little steam downstairs, Allen. Know what I mean?"

Beneath the White House was a subterranean labyrinth of winding tunnels and hidden vaults. An enormous Negro soldier, his chest bedecked in medals led the somber ensemble of men through the corridors. He directed the focused beam of light from a ship's lantern this way and that until the group arrived at a metal door, brown with rust and secured with a large padlock.

Once inside the dank, gloomy room, the president removed his jacket and pushed up the sleeves of his shirt above the elbows. Johnson's forearms were heavily corded in thick cables of muscle.

The beam illuminated a large man, seated on a wooden chair behind a small table. On the table was a single sheet of stationary, detailing the wrongs that the man was accused of perpetrating, along with a signature line. It was unsigned.

"Ignite the torches!" ordered a lean, chisel faced White House Security man. He was of short height, wore a Union forage cap and spoke with an Irish brogue.

Johnson didn't trust Americans on his security team. He had a lot of Irishmen and Scots, but mostly Negro soldiers for his personal protection. But he did not in the main, trust anyone - not truly.

"You're going to sign that parchment by the time I'm done with you," stated Johnson, who was built like an artilleryman, adding, "it is right there, in front of you, now sign it – sign the damned thing!"

Without warning, the formidable looking man dressed in the uniform of an Army general exploded from the chair, knocking the small table with its stationary violently aside.

Reflexively two of the Negroes assigned to protect the president seized the powerful general by either arm as others stepped in front of the POTUS to shield him from the charge.

The general that stood before the president was equal in height and solidly built. He was hatless and the hair dark and combed. The beard likewise was dark and unblemished with gray. A heavily chewed cigar remained clenched between the straight, browned teeth as General Grant, sizing up the president, said, "Have them unhand me, and let us settle this as men."

"I'd like that," the president replied in his aristocratic, southern drawl, "unhand General Grant."

"This is the means by which I longed to obtain the signature confession – by beating it out of you," explained President Johnson, who interlocked his fingers and extended his arms forward, popping his knuckles.

"You are going to crawl on your knees to that piece of paper and sign it. Then afterward, if you kiss the toe of my shoe I might let you live," Johnson added softly.

"My arse! I'm guilty of nothing and we'll soon set things straight!" retorted Grant, shaking himself loose from the two black soldiers, both of whom wore the Medal of Honor.

The president walked confidently toward the general, his powerful hands opening and closing like those of a grappler in adrenaline fueled anticipation.

Grant swung his right arm in a powerful round house, missing Johnson's face by an inch as the president moved his head deftly aside like a prize fighter and rushed into Grant, grabbing him in a bear hug and smashing his forehead into the general's. President Johnson buried his face into the side of the stunned general's bearded face, biting off the lobe of Grant's left ear.

"Son of a slut! *Son of a fucking whore!*" shouted Grant, staggering back and putting both hands to his ruined ear in the moment Johnson had released him – released him intentionally, although this did not cross Grant's mind.

"Got that right!" laughed the president, wiping the blood from his mouth with the back of his thick right wrist.

"Now, fight!" commanded the president.

"No! Mr. President!" shouted Allen Pinkerton. "Don't! Don't kill him! Just make him sign the document!"

"Don't worry about me, you duplicit cur," responded General Grant to Allen Pinkerton.

"I'm not signing anything, but this tyrant's death warrant!" Grant threatened, locking eyes with President Johnson.

"Talk comes cheap, boy!" answered Johnson, adding, "I'm just getting started with you! This is going to feel sooooooo good!"

Grant rushed Johnson, who kicked him squarely in the groin and sent the husky man down, doubled and groaning onto the damp cobble stone floor.

"Not getting out of it that easily, you scoundrel!" laughed Johnson, easily picking Grant up from the floor and throwing him across the room to the wall, where the general slammed against it and then fell like a sack of wet horse feed to the dank floor.

Grant, enervated with the new found energy of one who realizes his life may be about to end, broke a wooden leg from the upturned turned table and wielded it like a billy club while approaching the president.

"Bring it on!" the president said, smiling.

Ulysses S. Grant swung the blunt force trauma instrument with all his might, in an arcing, crescent shaped movement. There were gasps from the spectators as Johnson seized Grant's wrist with one hand at the moment of impact and broke it.

Grant stood, bent double, clutching his broken right wrist. The stub of his cigar was clenched tightly between his teeth as he tried not to scream.

The cigar of Grant fell to the floor and he began screaming so hard that no sound came from his mouth. The cigar was an icon of the swaggering Grant, made famous in numerous photos. However, now, its chomped butt resembled little more than an obscene lump of fecal matter.

"Gosh! That felt good!" exclaimed Johnston, adding, "I feel like a new man! Pinkerton – get me a bottle!"

"You're going to sign that piece of paper now, General," stated Johnson, adding, "because if you don't I am going to beat you like a red headed stepson. Look at it this way, you get out of line again, with this sworn statement I can hang your ass.

"You try to spread lies and malicious rumors against me, steal my mail and hatch assassination conspiracies, well go right ahead; I have your name! I have your number! I have your neck in a noose! This is a letter of resignation and the confessions of all that you did!"

"I'll never sign!" choked Grant through tears.

"Hold on a second now, Ulysses! What an arrogant, *puerile* sounding name for you. The way you just got your ass whupped. Just like what almost happened at Shiloh. While Sherman was there taking the bullets that should've been for you - you were sleeping off a hangover on your floating command ship, the *Tigress!*

"I'll be back," continued President Johnson, "you had better hope that you have not succeeded in the sabotage of Custer's campaign."

"WHAT!?" responded General Grant.

"Lol!" replied Johnson. "Go ahead and play the smart boy."

Chapter Eight: Hanwi the Accursed

Meanwhile, far from the basement of the White House, an obdurate George Armstrong Custer was approaching his objective stealthily through the icy, yielding snow.

The Indian village lay situated on the extreme western side of the enormous Oklahoma Indian Territory alongside the ice clogged Washita River.

The Oklahoma Indian Territory was a huge parcel of land that had been purchased by the government of the United States from the Napoleonic Empire as part of the Louisiana Purchase.

The land had been set aside as a sort of "Indian Reserve" and was a place to relocate the tribes as the series of Indian removals initiated by President Andrew Jackson progressed in the east.

The Indian Territory was bordered to the south by Texas, to the east by Arkansas, to the north by Kansas and Missouri, to the west by New Mexico, Colorado and the Texas Panhandle.

It was originally intended that the Indian Territory be a sort of autonomous entity, and it may have developed that way – had not the majority of the tribes got mixed up in the US Civil War, most of them unwisely fighting for the Confederacy.

Be that as it may, the slow, carefully controlled nocturnal ride led by Custer was conducted in the intermittent, wan light of a pale moon. The moon would be occulted for several minutes by sluggish, moisture swollen clouds that moved like ghosts, propelled on their way by a subdued arctic wind which would gain strength at once when the sun arose.

There was a surreal witch-like atmosphere that embellished the aberrant, pastoral setting. The mise en scène was enhanced and the landscape made eerie and cryptic when the clouds opened briefly, and moon beams flooded the vast, frozen panorama.

It was said by the Sioux and Cheyenne, that Hanwi the Accursed - the Sioux Goddess of the Moon held sway over the night-lands, when the moon was full and cast shadows on the forested hills wherein resided the mysteries of things unguessed.

They said that down through the cloud breaks gazed Hanwi the Accursed, on that fateful night. The tribal elders say that she looked onto the slumbering villages that lined the Washita River. During these moments, Hanwi would spill her aura onto the frozen lands; it was a terrain gilded with primordial shattered forests of ice broken trees and shimmering ivory mantles of deep, frozen snow.

Hanwi was said to be a cold goddess, and that she had been indifferent to the threat that approached the dreaming village of Chief Black Kettle. They said she stood atop her lunar throne bare breasted and opened her arms, causing the clouds to break and the land to become iridescent. The old ones say the pale light reflected from ice crystals as though from a shining sea of diamonds beneath her lunar throne.

She was, they say, as icy as her countenance was exquisite and she stared down onto the Valley of the Washita. Turning her beautiful head with its magnificent mane of black lustrous hair to one side, she made a sweeping motion with her left arm and the clouds, fecund with near freezing moisture, moved away in all directions.

The old men and women who pass on the story say the facial muscles moved as her mouth formed ferocious words in deafening silence; spoken in the windless vacuum of the moon. The nebulous curtain of scudding snow clouds that had ensconced the village of Black Kettle now opened up and revealed it in all its vulnerability.

The clouds, pregnant with moisture gave birth to the blizzards which now surrounded a periphery of twenty-five miles. The clear, moonlit sky with its inverted bowl of stars that looked down on the village of Black Kettle could have been the eye of a hurricane.

Hanwi the Accursed, it is said, clenched her goddess hands into fists and extended them toward the Washita. It was with those fists that she made a slow, turning, grinding motion. The muscles of her shoulders bunched as she dug her chin into her collar bone and looked down upon the developing scene below with stygian eyes.

Her face, it is said, was contorted into a visage of unfathomable antipathy toward the Sioux and Cheyenne; she was enraged at the warriors who had forsaken their race and taken to wife so many fair-skinned daughters of the trespassers.

Within the ice palace haunts of the depths of the gloomy tree lines moved indistinct, shaggy shapes. The deathly stillness of the night became at once animated with the crying of wolves, the yipping of coyotes and the cacophony of owls hooting in far-flung parliaments of feathered fury; they came swooping from the hollows of gnarled, ancient trees.

There were other sounds made in the surreal landscape, as well. These were sounds of the creaking that saddle leather makes when rubbed together, and metal shod hoofs crunching through frozen snow and contacting the frozen earth below. They followed the Indian trail located by Major Elliott into the Valley of the Washita ploddingly, inexorably.

Bloody Knife and the Osage trailers led point. They wore cavalry hats with tassel, as well as uniforms beneath the Army great coats. This was to distinguish them from the enemy. Closely behind followed Custer with his scouts.

The rest of the troops followed like specters within a winter purgatory, a half a mile to the rear. They halted at midnight in the icy, moonlit dreamland. The massively built geldings, grain fed war horses that weighed over 800 pounds, shied at the howling of the enormous packs of wolves so nearby.

Recognizing features from the terrain model, Custer saw that he was drawing nearer to his military objective. The former major general was keen-sensed and wired with adrenaline.

Leaving nothing to risk, Custer ordered the column to drop even further back - so as to prevent noise from alerting the tranquil village of Chief Black Kettle, which lay dreaming beneath the inverted bowl of stars which were scintillating in a prism of hues.

The sound of the hooves breaking through the frozen surface of the foot-deep snow carried over the moon limned surface of the icy precipitate in all directions, and up into the numbing, blue atmosphere where the stars blinked icily with frigid indifference.

The Arikawa scout Bloody Knife crested the slippery, ice covered hill, identified the slumbering village along with a huge herd of ponies and scooted back down the incline to inform Custer.

"Boy General!" whispered Bloody Knife.

"See large herd of horses in moonlight," Bloody Knife whispered. The Arikawa intimated to the Yellow Hair to follow him back up to the crest of the ridge.

"Lots bad Injuns down there. Heaps bad Injuns," reiterated Bloody Knife, pointing at the village with an outstretched arm.

Custer rolled to his left side and raising his right arm, signaled urgently to his officers to come forward to the topographical crest; he wanted them to assay the lay of the land and the location of the enemy. Then the Yellow Hair reiterated to each officer their part in the pending attack...

Down below, in the Valley of the Washita the sleeping village of Black Kettle lay nestled in buffalo hide tepees. The smell of wood smoke emanated from the burnt fuel of the hearth fires and issued from openings in the top of the conical tents; smoke made white by the intense freezing atmospheric temperature that hovered at zero degrees Fahrenheit.

The tenuous smoke columns rose lazily, curling into the twinkling blanket of stars that blinked and sparkled malevolently overhead in the icy, moonlit winter sky.

Two hundred warriors wearing bear and wolf skin furs had returned several nights before from a successful raid on isolated settlements in the Kansas frontier, having acquired a number of white female and child captives.

The successful braves had celebrated with a scalp dance, leaping and cavorting like demons, hideously prancing around roaring bonfires to the metronome beat of thundering war drums.

Black Kettle remained uneasily within his tepee during the festivities, wanting to have no part of it. Nor was he alone in his consternation with the warlike depredations of his young warriors. Chief Little Rock too, was frustrated at his lack of ability to restrain the young braves, who he felt had acted irresponsibly.

Dancers tied themselves to one another with cords of rawhide. They had been swapping off and bartering for the white captives while the war drums rumbled a deadly beat from dusk to dawn.

Although peace loving, soldier fearing Chief Black Kettle and his second in command, Little Rock did not like this, there was nothing they could do about it. They continued to abstain from the scalp dance, out of worry – and they needed to be worried.

The sixty-five-year-old Black Kettle, paranoid that the Army was everywhere, vowed to relocate the village at the first opportunity. Black Kettle and Little Rock both had cause for their paranoia, following the Sand Creek Massacre by the Army and white vigilantes in Southern Colorado during late November 1864.

The fact that Black Kettle and Little Rock could not stop their young braves from going on war parties any better now, than in 1864, was a continual source of bewilderment to both of the aged, pacifistic chiefs.

In part, they lay blame on the Dog Soldiers; renegade Cheyenne outcasts who continually exerted a charismatic spell over the restless young men of the village.

The horrific winter conditions had paralyzed the village, confining all but the war parties to the warm interiors of their tepees. Nevertheless, Black Kettle had resolved to relocate the village the following day. He could put it off no longer. He intuitively knew that *the Army would attack at any time.*

The orange-red bed of coals that rested in the fire pit cast a dull glow within the tepee of Black Kettle. Beneath the buffalo hide blanket Black Kettle's wife rested her head on his flabby chest.

Seeming to have a mind of its own, Black Kettle's scarred hand snuck its way into the crevasse of his much younger wife's firm behind, while outside a bitterly cold wind howled suddenly like a Valkyrie through the lifeless tree branches and caused the tepee to shudder.

In the Valley of the Washita, Cheyenne, Arapaho, Apache and Kiowa encampments contained tens of thousands of warriors and extended some twenty-five miles up the Washita River.

This vital intelligence was unknown to the determined Yellow Hair, who watched the unsuspecting village through squinted eyes and chattering, white teeth.

Chapter Nine: Big Top!

Meanwhile, to the east, on the outskirts of civilization and in another world almost, the stalled arctic air mass had delayed the Grim Family Circus for days. Only now – during a lull of stable weather did the circus approach its destination – Fort Dodge, Kansas.

A traveling circus generally would be a small affair consisting of a large nuclear family and comprising one, or perhaps, two wagons. Usually, feats of strength, limited acrobatics, and tricks of illusion were all that a transient, small frontier circus had to offer.

Since the affair was held out of doors in the open air, tickets were not sold, and fees were not set, per se; an offering plate such as used in tent revivals would be passed about as a means of collecting revenue.

The appearance of a truly professional circus which performed in an enormous canvas tent was a rare event in any frontier town, but especially so in far flung Fort Dodge, Kansas; thrust as it was like a soldier's knife deep into the lean underbelly of the American West.

This was a huge circus by frontier standards – by any standards –and the entertainment deprived population of Fort Dodge eagerly paid their fifteen cents to enter the massive canvas tent.

The locals, while escaping the cold, bitter wind, would enter into a convoluted world of artistic fairytale fantasy embellished with the pastels of lethal reality.

Although only a one ring circus, the tent was copious in size to accommodate sell-out crowds that flocked in from many miles around, whether come hellish drought or knee-deep snow.

The singular ring that lay one hundred feet beneath the dome of the big top measured some forty-two feet in circumference. Another fifteen feet or so of ground surrounded it before being abutted by the rows of wooden foldout chairs and benches.

Instead of the tent being formed with four poles in a single line as was the custom in the United States, it was supported instead with the poles forming a square, like in Europe. This was done so that more space was afforded for the spectators around the single ring.

As in Europe, the circus would retire for the winter months, its employees tending to personal matters and scattering far and wide across the country. A skeleton crew of essential personnel maintained the animals far to the south, in Sarasota, Florida.

This would be the last performance for the season; the schedule had been set earlier in the year and the unseasonal cold front had been unanticipated. The Grim Family Circus was behind schedule as a result. Nevertheless, the mantra of the circus was: *"THE SHOW MUST GO ON!"*

The Grims had hosted a garish exhibition, in the form of a promotional parade promulgating their anticipated arrival.

The ensemble at once connoted a triumphal Roman victory parade in which dangerous animals from distant lands were displayed in a moving procession akin to a military march. Crowds of onlookers thronged either side of the moving caravan. This display of wood and steel, of man and beast, and of angel and demon evoked grandiose cheers and curiosity which would seem incongruous to a man or woman of culture, who might have simply been passing through; the townspeople of Fort Dodge represented the dregs of society. The Grim Family Circus retinue was stretched along the main street of the army frontier town of Fort Dodge and made its way slowly to the icy, snow choked circus field a mile from the train station.

Equestrians caracoling on horseback, acrobats performing somersaults, and clowns skillfully juggling made up part of the retinue.

Behind them came the lumbering Conestoga wagons with the animal cages.

Big cats, Bengal tigers eight feet long and weighing a thousand pounds lunged at the shrieking spectators that lined the garbage strewn, snow covered dirt road that served as Fort Dodge's main street. From the humongous paws extended lethal retractable claws measuring six inches in length as the cats attempted to reach through the bars and pull horrified spectators into the cage.

The thrumming of loud, hollow percussions drummed from the fleshy human-like hands of six-foot-tall, six-hundred-pound silver back gorillas. The manlike beasts pummeled their chests with powerful staccato bursts and charged at the cages, rattling and shaking the rusted bars as they tried to bend them open with their oversized arms.

The apes were larger than their plant eating brethren in the African jungle, owing to the unnatural diet of red meat their keepers fed them. The manlike apes bared their yellow teeth and locked their bloodshot eyes fiercely with the terrified eyes of the spectators.

The Grims were a prominent circus family that had immigrated from war torn Europe during the early part of the century and had managed, through astute business acumen along with high risk venues, to stay afloat. More than that, they were making money – steamer chests full of green backs.

The Grim Circus would appear for a one-week hiatus in some God-forsaken frontier town and be gone like a zephyr the next.

The intrigues that went on within the world of the big top transpired unnoticed by the bloodthirsty public, who were enthralled and enjoyed the cathartic effect provided by the murderous feats of daring that often ended tragically.

The circus big top of the 19th Century Old West was a murky, sordid biosphere of duplicity, infidelity and murder.

Elizabeth and Margaret Custer watched enthralled, as two acrobats fenced in a death match using épées skillfully on the tight rope sixty feet above a murderous bed of knives.

The men were competitors for the same lusty dark-haired woman and had agreed to the duel on the tight rope according to preconditions set by the salacious ringmaster.

The ringmaster went by the name of Salazar – although no one knew his true name. He was a tall, thin, evil looking man and wore a bright scarlet tailcoat with gold trim - akin to that worn by British Redcoats during the Revolutionary War. Although contemporary for the time, the black felt top hat looked out of place atop the high forehead of the circus orchestrator.

A disquieting malevolence emanated from the ringmaster whose face was jaundiced, sunken, and made more sinister by a pair of slate eyes, set far back, of which the sclera was yellow. The bad teeth were broken and crowded together behind the thin lips of the broad mouth. Whenever the ringmaster smiled, it was done in a sneering way.

The ringmaster smiled quickly, too often and the smirk exuded insincerity from the cadaverous countenance.

Having been raised in the circus, this was a ruthless man of conniving skill and was a predator who sought to profit from the duel. The ringmaster would make a fortune in bets from among the circus performers and the local nobility indigenous to the entire metropolitan statistical area to which Fort Dodge was a nexus.

There were no safety lines attached to the two combatants who wore thin, flexible leather soled slippers very much similar to the leather moccasins worn by Native Americans. These specialty shoes allowed the sword fighters' feet to almost grasp the rope in a simian-like curving motion.

The young men – both in their mid-twenties were lean, muscular, and wearing tights. The contours of their ropey muscles were highlighted by shadow in the wan light of the circus tent as they thrusted and parried adroitly.

These were not the urgent thrusting and riposting attacks accompanied by dance like foot motion which took the contestants forward and back several feet.

This work was subtle and cautious, the gentle bouncing of the tightly stretched hemp rope added to the duel a balancing act in which a fall would prove calamitous.

The blood thirsty spectators were enraptured and oooohed and ahhhhed as the combatants sometimes wavered in their balance, sixty feet above the waiting bed of sharpened, sullen knives.

The two acrobats were dark haired and swarthy, of the same medium height and Mediterranean good looks, suggesting Italian pedigree. That they appeared non-dissimilar was not by chance; for they were identical twins.

As is the case with many identical twins, they wore the same clothing, favored the same food - and were attracted to the same woman - like moths to a flame.

"Do you suppose the urgent ripostes of their épées suggest that they compete to honor a young Lady?" Margaret asked Libbie Custer who studied the competitors with a discerning eye.

Libbie had been instructed in the art of fencing while at school and was considered to be a champion in the use of the weapon. She appreciated the skill exhibited and the fond memories that were evoked. Elizabeth also enjoyed the distraction from the boredom of garrison life that the death match provided.

"Yes, Margaret. Such a display of skill is for the benefit of a particular admirer of skillful swordplay. The object of their passion is gynic, and to be seen there –

standing anxiously beside the concession stand. She is a flyer with the trapeze performance scheduled for later today," answered Libbie Custer.

"Oh, and what a vixen she is, Libbie!" exclaimed Margaret, adding, "I suspect this is neither the first nor the last duel for the ardor of that rapacious heartthrob!"

"But in the final analyses they're just men, Margaret – animals," answered Libbie, "they're only good for one thing – alimony! Likely the baser of the two hoodlums will have more than his wounds tended by that doxy aerialist tonight," scowled Elizabeth.

"Just like out of the Old Testament, Libbie; brother against brother; Cain and Abel – but these acrobatic duelists are twins!" responded Margaret, edging closer to Libbie, leaning into her with the insincere pretext of seeking warmth in the cold tent.

A small band played drums and cymbals, maintaining a subdued tempo while awaiting one of the duelists to plummet like an Icarus onto the bed of knives below, the blades of which reflected the subdued light.

Margaret Custer was wearing a burgundy colored Victorian jacket unbuttoned near the bust line. Her skirt was matching, and she was seated to Elizabeth's left. The long-sleeved jacket, along with the corset beneath it, imparted a waspish, hourglass figure to the sister of the Boy General.

Libbie on the other hand, was attired in a brightly colored bustle dress plastered with happy imageries of cheerful, floral designs. Her long, auburn colored hair was half tied in a loose bun with side swept bangs that enhanced the classical features of her attractive face.

The rope was stretched taught yet flexed perceptibly toward the center where the two acrobats contended for the raven haired, olive skinned beauty named Delilah.

Delilah was attired in the tight-fitting leotard of a trapeze acrobat that hid little and showed much. Her firm, rounded gluteal muscles flexed and relaxed while she shifted her weight from one leg to the other and watched the contest with avidity.

Delilah had been born into the circus, her mother having been a Gypsy floor tumbler and sword swallower. Her father had been a fire eater and had died young, some said the mother had placed a scorpion in the man's shirt before he dressed, causing him to reflexively inhale the flame during a performance.

Nevertheless, Delilah was a part of the circus family. It seemed that no matter which circus she signed on with, she was the focus of ardor. If that meant violent struggles to win her passion, it was all part of an ephemeral life to her – and immortal death…

The living desideratum of passion beheld the spectacle through long, full, fluttering eyelashes. The eyelashes' bellicose appearance was enhanced by virtue of the application of mascara composed of lampblack, ash and elderberry juice.

The violent imageries of the thrusting, parrying competitors was absorbed into the soulless dark pools of stygian eyes. The pupils of Delilah were dilated with belladonna, in the fashion of Italian women to make them more captivating to their paramours.

The acrobatic Delilah was muscular from years on the trapeze and had matured short and curvy in stature. She covered her face with her hands while peeking nervously through her strong fingers at the épées that probed carefully, like long thick instruments of passion, seeking entry into yielding flesh.

The épée was a fencing sword of nearly three feet in length and weighing a little more than a pound and a half. The blood grooved, three-sided steel blade was flexible and had its origins in the earlier "small sword" – a derivative of the rapier. At the base of the evil weapon adjoining the full tanged handle was a flared bell guard to protect the hand.

Dueling to the death had for the most part fallen out of favor, and hence the épée was used primarily in sport and had a ball affixed to the tip of the weapon to prevent injury. Popular as a "1st blood" dueling weapon, the ball was removed in the duels in which the drawing of blood was the object.

In this contest of passion, naturally, the ball had been removed from the whip-like fencing swords which the wielders parried and thrust at each other.

The sword fighters were careful to maintain their lead foot beneath them. They used their bell guards to protect their forearms as they tried to balance on the constantly flexing, tensioned rope.

The official rules of fighting using an épée were vastly less restrictive and permitted the entire body to be used as a target, hence fencing with a foil or saber was preferred by many, in that the allowable target areas were restricted.

Bright red blood oozed lazily from superficial cuts but issued in fine, threadlike jets of ocher from the deeper lacerations. The audience gasped and awed with each surgical thrust which the Italian born twins delivered to each other, while at the same time tottering in their precarious balance.

They were named Romulus and Remus by their circus acrobat parents and were indistinguishable from each other – even by the circus women who knew them intimately.

Twins who survived as a set into adulthood were the exception rather than the rule during the 19th Century, when infant mortality ran about 218 deaths per 1,000 births.

The perils that subtracted from the sum of children that would enter adulthood were enormous as they ran a minefield of diseases and accidents. Even stepping on a rusty nail was a death sentence.

"Son of a whore!" exclaimed Romulus as he spat the distance to his brother's face, temporarily blurring his opponent's eyesight – his brother did not blink, but kept his eyes steadily on his determined, obdurate sibling.

"You speak true!" retorted Remus, who arched his spinal column as he leaned back precariously to avoid the perforating thrust of the épée aimed with the purpose of deflating his diaphragm.

In evading the épée, Remus was leaning too far back, and he lost his balance. Holding his sword, he waved both arms like some fool as though he could fly. Despite the frenetic waving of his upper extremities, which evoked exclamations of awe from the mesmerized spectators below, Remus could not maintain his balance. Over the damned rope he went, dropping his épée and grabbing for dear life onto the tight rope with the strength of both calloused hands.

In the act of arresting his fall, Remus had seized the hemp rope fiercely. The acrobat remained obstinate in his refusal to accede to the pleas of gravity. His adamancy precipitated the robust flexing and rebounding of the tightrope - as though it were an enormous guitar string.

And so, it was then Romulus who found himself balancing desperately, tottering wildly and flailing his beefy arms. Then, careening sideways on one foot with the other held in the air perpendicularly, he dropped his épée like a complete idiot.

It was during the act of plunging toward catastrophe that Romulus had grabbed the tight wire fiercely, with both fleshy hands when he heard the crowd explode into gasps of horror, astonishment and surprise.

The appreciation of the daring display of bravado was manifested in a standing ovation of sustained applause.

Margaret grabbed Libbie's wrist, squirming in her seat. She was clearly ecstatic with excitement and spilled her paper bag of popcorn onto the wet ground.

"Look at them fight, Libbie!" extolled Margie.

"This program appears to be choreographed for the entertainment of young ladies," answered Libbie.

"Why do you say that?" asked Margie.

"Because look how they sweat, Margaret," answered Libbie.

"See how their muscles strain through those obscene tights they call leotards? Of course, this is draw for the fairer sex!

"The women cajole their husbands and lovers into augmenting the attendance of the circus, and through this means the circus performers sustain their gypsy-like existence," explained Libbie impatiently.

"Oh look, Libbie!" exclaimed Margaret.

"They are advancing toward each other hand over hand on the tight rope, each with a mind to send the other on a fatal plunge onto the waiting bed of knives!" exclaimed Margaret, fascinated at the lethal determination of the competitors.

The tendons stood out on the backs of the thick, muscular hands of the contenders as they gripped the rough fibers of the heavy hemp rope. They advanced toward one another, passing one hand over the other hand, moving to within kicking distance. Sweat ran dripping from their grimacing faces and fell from their noses and chins onto the bed of rusting knives sixty feet below.

"Look how the acrobats twist and writhe like contortionists, Libbie – oh look he kicked his brother in the most unnamable of places! They are going for the family jewels!" shouted Margaret enthusiastically.

"Control yourself, Margaret. Or you will draw attention to us and appear unladylike," warned Libbie.

But Libbie's admonition could scarcely be heard above the tumultuous roaring applause of the crowd that seethed and eddied far below the swinging, kicking brothers.

The spectacle was comparable to the spurring of fighting cocks as the combatants rose and fell with the bouncing rebounds of the tight rope.

"Unnnngh!" grunted Remus, exhaling his air when his brother had kicked into the taut abdomen. Remus had doubled up reflexively, releasing the rope and grabbing onto his brother's legs as he fell.

They hung there, suspended above the bed of knives waiting patiently sixty feet below; Romulus clinging for life to the tight wire, supporting the weight of both himself and his twin brother.

"I almost can't bear to watch! What do you anticipate will happen next, Libbie?" Margaret's eyes were not on the dueling acrobats; they were fixated on the fleshy mounds of her sister in law. Libbie's endowments were pushed high up by the tight, iron maiden fitting corset, exaggerating the cleavage and making the apple sized globes appear much larger than they were.

Romulus writhed like a serpent, trying to shake Remus loose. Suddenly his leotard tights slid down and pulled off, Remus along with them.

The crowd's roaring approval manifested itself in a standing ovation once again as Remus plunged toward the bed of sentient blades.

The falling trapeze artist glanced instinctively at the audience and saw a woman staring at the blessings that protruded from above another woman's upper torso. One was wearing a brightly colored bustle dress. Then everything went blindingly white...

The audience's thunderous applause had transcended to raucous laughter as they gazed and pointed at the surviving twin and winner of the contest. With his leotard pants torn off, his truncheon swung lazily as the tight rope bounced up and down.

Delilah swooned and had to be assisted to another tent.

Chapter Ten: "Sound the Attack!"

No one with the 7th Cavalry was aware of the Grim Family Circus, nor of the depraved, entertainment deprived audience that fed itself off of the Roman Holidays type atmosphere of the Big Top at far away Fort Dodge, in the Weird, Weird, West.

Instead, the 7th Cavalry had its own performance to play beneath a different canopy altogether; a canopy evinced in an icy, enormous, inverted bowl of twinkling stars.

Custer had ordered his men to doff their overcoats and haversacks onto the snow prior to advancing to the attack position. Whether this demonstrated sound judgement or not is open to debate. But they did it.

The lieutenant colonel was at the attack position. As the sergeants and corporals prepared their men, the Yellow Hair conferred with the officers of his assault element.

The Yellow Hair was discussing up to the moment, final details, when he noticed an anomaly in the predawn sky. His officers saw it at the same time. It rose distinctly above the hillsides that were aglow in the yellow wash of the ghostly moonlight.

"What manner of phenomena is that?" the Boy General inquired of his cadre. "Is it a signal flare? I gave no such order!"

Slowly the gleaming sphere rose above a hill, manifesting itself as a flaming, boiling, iridescent orb of gold. It continued to ascend, growing in size. Then it began to move slowly, while its colors changed violently in a kaleidoscope of convoluted, oscillating spectrums.

"It seems as though we have been discovered!" exclaimed the exasperated Boy General.

"See how it has stopped and hangs there!" exclaimed one of the officers.

"Indeed! What phenomena! Something is not right, nothing good portends of this!" replied Custer.

Suddenly a rifle shot rang defiantly from the village, directed at the glowing orb, more shots rang out as the Cheyenne, enraged at the appearance of the glowing sphere began exploding from their tepees in order to take it under fire.

Their faces were misshapen expressions of outrage, the impression imparted was made more terrifying by the war paint that bedaubed their belligerent features.

With each impact of a bullet, the orb would brighten, and the hues scintillate in a convolution of colors.

"Sound the attack!" ordered Custer.

Immediately the band began playing "Garry Owen." The boisterous melody was answered by roars of approval from all sides by the soldiers ensconced in their attack positions.

All hell broke loose as the attack began. No one noticed that the glowing, pulsating object had vanished from sight…

The icy morning air was ripped by multiple volleys of rifle shot from the edge of the village. Cooke's sharpshooters answered with carefully aimed fire from their carbines.

The trumpeters sounded the stirring notes of the "Charge," and at almost the same time the wind instruments playing the tune Garry Owen began to freeze up; the saliva of the musicians turning to ice and rendering the instruments mute.

Ever since the Battle of the Washita, Garry Owen, which had its origins in Ireland as a drinking song, has been the regimental song of the 7th Cavalry. Within seconds 800 troopers were thundering into one of the most contentious and controversial battles in United States military history.

 "Soldiers!" cried the village inhabitants.

The warriors who spilled from their tepees and took the glowing orb under fire were of above average height. Their jet-black hair was worn in twin pony tails, tightly braided. The braids were secured with rawhide thongs, then sheathed beaver skin sock-like coverings. Not having had time to dress warmly, some wore knee length war shirts made of buckskin and captured cavalry trousers.

Hamilton and West's squadrons were the first to enter the awakened village, firing wildly as they rode through it. The once furry paunch of Hamilton's stomach had been rubbed smooth from the march and it jiggled as he bounced violently in the McClellan saddle.

Enraged, Black Kettle ran like a startled mountain lion from his tepee and mounted his unsaddled horse, unclothed and bareback. The cursing, peace loving chief headed for the Washita River at a full gallop through the iced snow. He used the reigns to whip the neck of the horse from side to side as he yelled to spur it on.

Black Kettle tilted his head back and shouted in anger as he was hit multiple times in the back.

Long, thick, braided hair shocked with gray extended half way down the venerated chief's back. The braids lifted and swung from side to side in slow motion as he shook his head and roared with each bullet wound.

The hair was parted in the middle of a head which sloped back abruptly – almost like that of a microcephalic individual. Black, marble eyes overhung with heavy epicanthic folds stared upward into the fading stars. The high set cheekbones were the defining feature of the face, contorted in rage. The nose was quashed in, from having been broken long ago. The thin lips were pulled back from worn, tobacco stained teeth in sneering defiance of the hail of bullets snapping all around him.

Grabbing at the gaping exit wounds which spurted geysers of steaming blood from his chest, his curses were blood choked epitaphs as he plunged headfirst into the icy cold embrace of the freezing water.

Scores of Cheyenne were running into the freezing water, heavily armed and firing from the riverbank.

A group of thirty others were entering the partially frozen river and navigating between huge boulders of floating ice from which ricocheted bullets. Among some of the survivors climbing onto the other side of the riverbank was the leader of the group of thirty warriors who sought to escape from the soldiers. As they clambered onto the opposite bank, water froze on their clothing.

The leader's head was shaven entirely except for a scalp lock near the top of his head, to which a tail feather from an immature golden eagle was affixed. The impression conveyed by the scalplock made the piranha- like face of the shivering headman even more determined looking.

The obsidian, shark-like eyes darted perceptively in all directions. When he halted the group, everyone went to their knee and surveyed their surroundings. Then cagily he resumed his cautious advance toward the treeline.

The septum of the nose had been pierced and a brass bullet shell was stuck through either side of it. The warrior's leather war shirt and buckskin trousers had frozen and become stiff, as had a magnificent triple hair pipe war vest. A captured cavalry belt supported a black leather flap holster with a Colt 1860 – its powder wet. The high-topped moccasins that extended up beneath the knees were saturated with water and had frozen stiff.

When the iceman began edging forward again, he was followed by twenty-nine tall, powerfully built warriors, who looked from right to left. Water had frozen almost immediately on their clothing. But nevertheless, they had escaped from the village of Black Kettle and were now several miles away from the shooting.

The dark, observant eyes penetrated piercingly into the iced, white treelines that offered sanctuary and the opportunity to build a fire. They desperately needed to thaw and dry their clothing. All carried repeating rifles. They were silent as they approached another belt of forest, distancing themselves from the cataclysm that had befallen their village.

he headman in the front of the column froze. He was of average height and middle aged, savvy in the ways of field-craft and hunting. He was a dangerous, desperate man and the tendons of his neck stood out suddenly as he turned his head to the right and stared directly at an old, fallen tree behind which he had heard someone cough.

A collar-necklace of mummified human fingers was tied loosely around his thick, bull neck. The overdeveloped biceps of the warrior strained against the frozen sleeves of the buckskin war shirt that resisted them. A cavalry belt held a leather scabbard containing a murderous hunting knife.

Although Cheyenne, he had European facial features and wore oversized, loop earrings made of copper beaten from spent bullet shells. He stood crouched while searching the length of the fallen tree for a moment, and then advanced toward where the cough originated. His rifle was held with both hands at waist height, muzzle pointing forward as he drew nearer the fallen tree. There was an audible click as the hammer was cocked back on the Spencer repeating rifle. His copper earrings swung with the motion of turning his head back to face his companions, nodding one way and then the other for them to fan to either side of the fallen tree.

He paused for a moment, uncertain as to whether to advance or have his friends do it. Suddenly, a skillful imitation of a whooping cough from behind the tree overcame his better judgement and prompted him to advance toward the source of the hoarse, barking cough.

He saw one of his companions; a man who wore a buffalo skin skull cap complete with a polished horn jutting upward from either side of the temples. From beneath this fur cap extended two braids of shoulder length black hair, wrapped in ermine socks. This man intimated that the curious leader should advance toward the tree. The other braves converged on the source of the cough, which had become incessant, shrill, and strident.

Had the braves bothered to look above them, into the trees, they would never have been trapped beneath the net that fell upon them.

Back at the village, soldiers entered tepees, pulling screaming women and children from beneath buffalo robes at gun point.

Custer entered a larger than normal tepee, confronting an elderly man underneath heavy buffalo skin blankets. The old man was with an almond eyed teenage beauty. This was none other than the venerable Chief Little Rock – the co-chief of the village who ruled it along with Black Kettle.

"Now I have you, Yellow Hair!" shouted Chief Little Rock, pointing a Colt Army Model 1860 .44 caliber revolver squarely at Custer's face. The chief, vigorous for a man in his 60s, thumbed back the hammer, causing the cylinder to rotate.

Custer stood frozen in place, not moving a muscle.

"Father," cooed the ravenous beauty beside the old man, "don't hurt him – he is for me."

She leaned into the chief, causing his aim to deviate, making him shoot high and right as the deafening discharge filled the tepee with gunsmoke.

"Monahsetah! You threw my aim off!" shouted Little Rock, pushing her away and thumbing back the hammer to get another shot.

"Kill him, Yellow Hair!" screamed Monahsetah, sitting up, completely disrobed beneath the bed of furs.

Custer's reaction was classical in the gun fighting sense. With his right hand he reached with lightning speed to the holster on his left hip in a magnificent, heart pounding rendition of the controversial "cross draw."

The Boy General did not bring the balanced Remington Model 1858 New Army to eye level. Instead, he fanned off a single shot from the hip, using the heel of his left hand.

The ball shaped bullet struck the old man solidly in the sternum at over 800 feet per second. The trajectory of the soft lead ball deviated slightly and exploded the man's heart. Then the next speeding slug hit the cursing man squarely in the forehead.

The widely spaced, onyx eyes drifted lazily from left to right in nystagmus as Chief Little Rock at first remained sitting up. His ears were decorated in many places and earrings made of beads and dentalium shells jiggled as he began to spasm. The unbroken nose hooked evilly. Suddenly the pacifistic chief collapsed backwards and began going into seizures; violently trembling in his death throws.

Monahsetah had determined to marry the Boy General within the selfsame moment that Custer had sent the bullet smashing into her father's wicked heart and thick forehead.

For several moments the tepee was filled with the rotten egg smell of spent black powder, and visibility was made more limited by the gunsmoke in the dimly lit structure.

The Boy General could hear his pulse pounding despite the ringing in his ears. The detonation from having fired his revolver within the tepee had been deafening.

The near-death experience was causing Custer to become nauseated and light headed. He began to hyperventilate and, leaning against the supporting pole inside the tepee, he fought down the panic attack that was assailing him.

The nubile woman was not encumbered with even a stitch as she flung the heavy blankets aside, covering Little Rock's face and his post mortem grin. She launched herself upon the Yellow Hair. She locked her arms around him in a fierce embrace born of concern for his well-being.

The hot embrace of the unclad woman confused the lieutenant colonel, as he tried to slow his racing heart and rapid breathing. The woman embraced him more fiercely and began grinding herself into the Boy

General as he tried to slow his galloping, out of control tachycardia.

The Yellow Hair concentrated with every fiber of his consciousness to not succumb to an incipient asthma attack. It was as though the air had no oxygen. He could not get his breath…

The woman was attempting to unbuckle the Boy General's trouser belt, pulling at it fiercely until it unfastened - as his face turned blue. Custer gasped for air like a fish hauled to the bank and left to die.

The woman seemed to curse as she struggled with the trousers now, yanking and pulling at them. The Lieutenant Colonel placed both of his hands on her smooth, tan shoulders to steady his balance as he looked up at the round hole in the ceiling of the tepee. He was forming an "O" with his lips as he tried breathing through them and slow his hyperventilation.

The Boy General felt his knees start to give way as the close call with his mortality threatened to overwhelm him.

"Leave Boy General 'lone!" ordered Bloody Knife, pulling Monahsetah off of him, "and put on clothes! You go with prisoners!"

Bloody Knife grabbed Custer and flung him through the opening of the tepee onto the snow and began caking the frozen moisture about his head and face, slowing the Boy General's breathing.

"Come back, Boy General! Come back to us!" implored Bloody Knife.

Gradually the light of recognition returned to the azul eyes of the Yellow Hair.

A hundred yards away from where Custer contended with the consequences of his close brush with death, Captain Meyers was hampered by heavy brush and fallen timbers.

Meyers' eyes darted from left to right, surveying the terrain. He cursed as he moved his men through the snow and to the right, crossing the freezing Washita River. He charged the village in wet, freezing clothes and met no resistance. Captain Meyers emerged at the sand bluffs to the south and was immediately taken under fierce fire by the Cheyenne.

Some of the Cheyenne were still armed with bows constructed of locust, hickory, and ash. The arrow shafts were often made of juniper and were slightly less than three feet long. More often these days the arrowheads were made of sharpened metal. The fletchings were made of practically any type of feather. The quivers usually consisted of beaver, foxes, and coyotes to ease the launch of an arrow every two to three seconds.

Lieutenant E.S. Godfrey took two platoons and began the difficult task of rounding up the half wild Indian herd of ponies. The ponies panicked at the scent of white men and were almost uncontrollable.

Major Elliott, overcome with initiative, chased after a group of fleeing Indians, composed entirely of women and children. Sergeant Major Walter Kennedy and eighteen men enthusiastically accompanied him.

"Here goes for a brevet or a coffin!" shouted Major Elliott to his entourage. He and his ensemble vanished forever from the village of Chief Black Kettle and into the annals of 7th Cavalry lore.

The 7th Cavalry's soldiers were setting fire to tepees in an operation akin to search and destroy, where a hamlet is searched and then put to the flame.

Meanwhile, inside the tepee of Chief Little Rock, the Yellow Hair examined unopened mail contained in the leather saddlebags of a slain horse courier. One of the saddle bags contained a thick stack of daguerreotypes.

Strewn all about the tepee were implements from murdered settlers' cabins. Then suddenly his attention was captured by imageries that he saw in the daguerreotypes.

'What's this? Lo and behold!" the statement was uttered in the exclamatory, which to all present enhanced the interest of what lay within the tome of photographic imageries.

The images seemed to hold the Boy General in a state of frozen animation. His straight, white teeth were constantly brushed and flossed, and they shone like those of a carnivorous predator which sees a threat and instinctively freezes in place.

Custer had doffed the badger skin hat in exasperation, unleashing a mop of yellow hair that was womanlike in its length. The wearing of hats had imparted a waviness to the dirty blond mane, and it fell languorously to the broad shoulders.

Custer could be mistaken for a younger man. The proud forehead, always protected from the sun by ridiculous, ostentatious, wide brimmed hats was smooth and unlined. Reddish blond eyebrows grew above cunning, blue eyes; eyes that were quick to perceive the import of the daguerreotypes. The eyes, it is said, are the windows into a man's soul. If this adage holds merit, his eyes were blue with bale fire at what they beheld.

The face of Custer was thin and rectangular, and made sinister as it frowned, chagrined at the photography. The jawline was tightly set in rage beneath the high cheek bones. The man's handsome features were offset by an overlarge, hooking nose which he tried to obfuscate with a grotesque, albeit popular walrus style mustache. The dark blond mustache was distinct from the goatee that Custer allowed to grow on his chin. The Yellow Hair's countenance was supported by a muscular, athletic neck.

Custer carefully thumbed through each of the page size daguerreotypes, slowly. His breath issued in twin columns of steam from his long, Gallic nose in the frigid air.

The Yellow Hair was at the entrance of Little Rock's tepee, where there was more light. The Cheyenne woman named Monahsetah was no longer present - having been clothed, then assimilated with the growing number of prisoners.

The vapor that was exhaled through Custer's nares reminded Bloody Knife of newspaper cartoons he had seen of steam breathed from the nostrils of enraged Spanish fighting bulls.

"Look like pictures of naked lady," offered Bloody Knife, edging closer to Custer, craning his neck to get a better look of the sensual white beauty performing lingual obeisance on a huge muscular Negro.

The black man's anatomy was so large that only a small portion of the shimmering glans of the globoid, sensitive crown could fit into the petite white woman's facial orifice.

Bloody Knife had never seen daguerreotypes of this nature before.

"Get the hell out of here, Bloody Knife! Get out, everyone!" shouted Custer, pulling the daguerreotypes in close to his coat, alarmed that prying eyes might discern the images on the daguerreotypes, might recognize the unclad woman who grasped the man's engorged stones with one dainty hand while holding the shaft of the man's massive endowment with the other.

Custer's eyes were narrowed in incredulity as the woman piped and fluted the distended, tumescent glans of the black man's enormous erectile organ. The ebon giant's straight, white teeth were exposed by bulbous lips pulled back in snarling ecstasy.

"Who was the rider from whom the war party stole these pictures!" Custer shouted futilely at the dead body of Chief Little Rock, who lay unresponsive beneath the blankets of animal skins.

The Boy General was dazed, and bewildered. He felt punch drunk and discombobulated. All at a time when he needed to focus his attention on the task at hand.

"How could she?" he asked himself. "I never knew, I never suspected – not in a thousand years!"

It was the sense of *betrayal* that assailed the Yellow Hair, rather than some sense of hurt feelings or broken heart.

It was her disloyalty and the violation of her vows that dug into him like the spurs of a Spanish picador digging at the flanks of a gored mount.

Custer placed the daguerreotypes back into the leather satchel and carefully secured it with a string of rawhide sewn onto the satchel, tying it in a double bowknot.

"Bloody Knife! *BLOODY KNIFE!!!*" Custer was sticking his head through the portal of the tent, calling to his trusted Arikawa scout.

130

"Yes, Boy General! Bloody Knife hear the Yellow Hair!" answered Bloody Knife, running through the stained blanket of frozen wintry precipitate, back to Little Rock's tepee, where he saw Custer stepping out onto the snow.

"Go get my photographer, Charles Scholten, and tell him I have a surprise for him! Do it now Bloody Knife –*NOW MOVE!*" Custer ordered his favorite scout, and probably best friend.

It was then, as his personal world lay shattered within the satchel that things suddenly became worse; four soldiers brought up Hamilton's body to Custer. The grandson of Alexander Hamilton had been shot through the heart. He'd been killed almost immediately at the head of his squadron during the initial assault. Captain Barnitz was wounded critically.

Many enlisted men were hit, and the tempo of firing had not decreased – on the contrary - it was growing, as thousands more Indians rushed from neighboring villages like angry hornets to assist the doomed village of Black Kettle.

They lashed at their war painted ponies guiding them toward the 7th Cavalry. The braves came on without fear and at an almost full gallop despite the snow. The braves shook cattle bells, ringing them madly in order to spook the white men's cavalry horses.

The Cheyenne were putting up a better fight than anticipated. The odds were unequal, and Custer was rubbing the temples of his forehead with the fingers of both hands as he tried to think.

A mile away and increasing the distance was the determined Major Joel Elliott, sweating and breathing hard. Despite the dearth of ample clothing and the freezing temperature, the hot pursuit had the ragtag goggle of chasers rasping for air and sweating.

A Civil War hero, Major Joel Elliott, had been a Quaker and a fervent abolitionist who'd fallen out with his family when he'd enlisted as a private to fight for the Union during the recent Civil War. His pacifist family had angrily disowned him when he chose a uniform and a rifle instead of that of a Bible and a plow shear.

Elliott had been popular with many of the men when Custer was being court martialed, and some of the 7th Cavalry wished to see their likeable officer back in charge again. Custer had a lot of enemies within the 7th Cavalry, in part because of his egotistical personality, and also because he drove his men mercilessly. To his credit though, the Boy General also had his admirers, who respected the officer because he drove himself twice as hard as he did his men.

Elliott, along with his entourage of eighteen men and Sergeant Major Walter Kennedy had last been seen in pursuit of women and children to capture as prisoners. Then Elliott and his group went missing; they could not be accounted for during the worsening crisis.

Within the village of Black Kettle, the tempo was in high gear as the Indian ponies were rounded up. Twenty-five-year-old, whip thin 1st Lieutenant Edward S. Godfrey was of average height and fair complexion. The Civil War veteran with his men rounded up 800 ponies and had heard a maelstrom of rifle fire from the direction whence Elliott had vanished.

When Godfrey topped a bluff to see if he could espy Elliott, he saw instead tepees as far as the eye could see. He became alarmed and electrified as adrenaline pumped through constricting veins.

Emerging from the villages were thousands of winter clad warriors mounted on ponies which were painted with specific designs. Some of the images were horse hooves on the horses' flanks. Many had symbols of lightning and all had circles painted around their eyes. The Indians emerged circling like enraged bees in the distance as they spilled angrily from their hives.

Most of the Cheyenne were riding bareback, while others straddled saddles made of stretched buffalo hide stuffed with straw. Some had saddles ruthlessly taken from homesteads of slain settlers and ambushed cavalrymen.

The tree lines increasingly became enlivened, animated with rifle fire as Lt Godfrey came under growing attack.

Cheyenne, Sioux, Comanche and even Apache were appearing from anywhere that offered cover. Some of

133

the Indians would run toward the defenders in rushes on foot, while others remained behind rocks and trees, providing a suppressive, covering fire.

They were war whooping and firing repeating rifles from the hip as they ran through the snow from one area of cover to the next. The Cheyenne and Sioux, along with the Comanche and Apache came sprinting at an all-out run. Their braided black hair was swinging in pony tails. Their faces were covered in war paint of terrible imageries and it streaked as sweat ran down their faces - despite the freezing temperatures.

"Odd numbers! Lay down a suppressive fire! Even numbers withdraw," Lieutenant Godfrey had shouted as he controlled the retreat.

At the next defendable land feature, such as a knoll, ridgeline, or copse of trees, the even numbers would cover the withdrawal of the desperately firing odd numbers.

Godfrey left a subordinate temporarily in charge as he tried to make it back to the village to inform Custer of the developing situation.

Custer at all times demanded up to the moment information and was seldom ignorant of his tactical environment. He was irascible, prone to second guessing himself and would take unreasonable risks against high odds. But he was kept aware of what those odds were, more so than most field commanders.

It was then, that Bloody Knife announced himself at Chief Little Rock's tepee with the photographer, Charles Scholten.

"Boy General!" announced Bloody Knife.

"What is it that you want!?" snapped Custer. The words came in a rush from Boy General as he whirled to face Bloody Knife, tucking the leather satchel containing the daguerreotypes beneath his left armpit.

"Boy General! Bloody Knife bring Scholten for big surprise!"

The sinewy, muscular Indian brought the photographer Charles Scholten into the tepee and waited.

The Arikawa was an enigma to everyone who had any dealings with him – except for Custer. Bloody Knife's father was a Hunkpapa Sioux and his mother was Arikawa. He forsook feathers, jewelry and beads.

The Arikawa scout had the looks of a Spaniard and preferred the company of whites – dressing like them in every way he could and adopting their ways. His hard, dark irises were set in clear white eyes and were enhanced by the absence of epicanthic folds. The delicate facial features were accentuated with robust cheekbones that while high set, didn't detract from the man's features. A narrow nose resided above thin lips.

"Good! Stick around a minute, Bloody Knife. Fun's just getting started," exclaimed Custer, who added, "Scholten, come here for a second. I have a topic interest to present to you! Get your ass over here! *DO IT NOW!*" commanded Custer.

"What's the deal, General?" asked Charles Scholton, Custer's photographer, "You want me to get a photo of the action?"

"You've captured plenty of action with your damned camera, haven't you, boy!" growled Custer, unsheathing his razor-sharp carbide steel hunting knife. "Well -*SURPRISE!!!*"

The knife cut cleanly through palm of Scholten's extended left hand as he attempted to shield his neck from the murderous instrument of his demise.

The upper half of the hand fell twitching spasmodically to the animal skins that covered the ground beneath the tent.

The momentum of the vicious swipe of the silvery blade had carried through and cut the man's throat, completely severing the trachea.

"Boy General kill picture man!" complimented Bloody Knife, his obsidian eyes became alive. His normally stoic features were animated by a half smile at the scene that had just unfolded before him.

"Quickly! Help me cover him with the blankets!" ordered the Yellow Hair.

No sooner had Custer and Bloody Knife hidden the treacherous photographer beneath the blankets of animal skins than their murderous conclave risked discovery; unbeknownst to them, the capable Lieutenant Godfrey was making his way to Custer with an urgent situation report.

"Hurry, Bloody Knife and get the scouts together. We're getting out of here as soon as possible," the Yellow Hair ordered. His sentence came in a rush of words.

"The Indians," shouted Godfrey as Bloody Knife pushed past him, "they are attacking en masse! You said that you wanted to be told!"

"Ah, Yes! Well how about that! How the hell bad is it now?" responded the Yellow Hair as he quickly regained his composure; he felt better now – better than he had ever felt in his entire life.

"What is the situation?" restated Custer calmly.

Lieutenant Godfrey's response came in a torrent of words as the crescendo of rifle fire increased exponentially with the arrival of the numerous, uncoordinated bands of warriors from Cheyenne, Arapaho, Comanche, Apache tribes. None of the indigenous warriors were subordinate to anyone. All were intent on getting in on the kill.

The chiefs did not recognize a singular leader amongst their numbers. They were all enormous men in flowing war bonnets – many were mounted on Appaloosas. All of their faces were slathered in war paint.

They wore leather chaps and mismatched clothing beneath the heavy buffalo skin coats. They hurled insults at their men, calling them girls. Without warning, from one of the tree lines, an attack force erupted from the icy vaults and rushed the firing soldiers. Mounted chiefs slid off of ponies which had orbs painted around both eyes and human hands painted on the flanks. They ran dodging behind rocks and trees as they worked their way in closer to Black Kettle's village. Some of the Indians were not wearing heavy coats but wore buckskin war shirts instead – despite the cold. The pockets were filled with ammunition.

"There are villages and encampments as far as the eye can see," answered Godfrey, elaborating, "the villages are large, consisting of hundreds of tepees, and extend around the river's bend. There are large contingents of mounted warriors riding through the snow and headed this way. Thousands. Perhaps ten thousand."

1st Lieutenant Godfrey's wolverine cap was pulled down over his ears, but he still shivered; the issued coats had been ordered cached prior to the attack so as to not encumber the men. As a result, Godfrey shivered involuntarily as he saw the jawline of the Yellow Hair tighten and the blond countenance smile in a visage of joviality despite the worsening situation.

138

"I am worried about Major Elliott also," Godfrey added. "He disappeared into the woods, where the glowing orb seemed to hang in the air."

Lieutenant Godfrey briefly described in clear, concise language the firing which he had heard; he thought it might be where Elliott was.

"There was a big fire fight, General – it sounded like several hundred rifles. A lot of Henrys. All that firing took place where Elliott disappeared. They're probably in real trouble and need our help!"

Custer speculated, then replied, "No, I don't think so. Lt. Colonel Meyers has been down there all morning and in fact would have reported it. And don't worry about the odds – they're a million to one against us! *And they don't stand a chance!*"

"Boy General!" shouted Bloody Knife as he re-entered the tepee. "Bad Injuns on all ridges surrounding valley! Lieutenant Bell come! He bring ammo wagons! Bad Injuns steal soldiers' coats and haversacks!"

Hundreds of howling, dismounted braves were running between the trees as they fired. Some were dressed in a mismatch of captured Army uniforms and clothing of murdered settlers. Some of the warriors even wore dresses beneath heavy buffalo skin coats. The florid, hybrid clothing apparel added a kaleidoscope of color to the growing number of warriors. This seething, tinctured panoply of garish pigmentation was converging into a sentient, multihued killing entity.

"Godfrey – kill all of the village's Indian ponies! Get on it!" commanded the former general.

"Bugler! Sound Officers' Call!" ordered Custer, adding, *"We're going to attack!"*

"Meyers, take charge of the prisoners and prepare to head for Camp Supply. When you make ready the prisoners, see that no harm becomes them," continued Lt. Col. Custer. "Make sure of that personally," Custer added.

"Bloody Knife, grab the Osage scouts and order them to prepare to lead the way out of here!" shouted Custer above the cacophony of gunfire and screaming horses.

"Listen up, gentlemen! While the camp prepares to pick up and move, we're going up to that treeline and we're going to clear it out! Form your men into companies. *NOW, LET'S DO IT!!!"*

The surrealistic scene could have been taken right from Dante's Inferno as Custer led the charge against the thousands of leaderless Native Americans, who broke and fled like the beaten rebels near the end of the Civil War at the Battle of Sailor's Creek, where it is said that General Lee cried.

The small, heavily armed team of Osage scouts was dressed in cavalry attire to prevent them from being mistaken for hostiles. Carefully, they rode through the gelid white blanket on their mounts to prepare the way.

Chaos ensued as the Indian ponies, a mismatched conglomeration of short horses which reflected a multitude of color patterns and pedigrees, were shot in all manner of places vital to their survival.

The ponies ran pell-mell through the alabaster carpet of arctic precipitation; neighing and spraying steaming jets of blood profusely in crimson geysers. From that time on the Cheyenne would forever call this incident "The Blood Moon."

Following Custer's return to the camp of Chief Black Kettle, Captain Benteen urgently confronted Lieutenant Colonel Custer, grabbing him by the sleeve of the coat.

"You can't leave Elliott back there," Benteen told Custer. Then seeing the Boy General had already, in fact, made up his mind to do so, Benteen boldly added, "you bastard!"

Custer wasn't perturbed by Benteen's invective.

Assigned to the 7th Cavalry in July 1866, thirty-three-year-old Captain Frederick W. Benteen was doggedly pleading with the Yellow Hair to send out a strong detail to search for Major Elliott.

"Let me lead it! Let me go find him – *FOR THE LOVE OF GOD!!!*" implored Captain Benteen.

Captain Frederick Benteen was of medium height and build. A thick mop of greying hair reigned in dignity atop a high forehead and leprechaun face. A neatly manicured moustache lay beneath a short, straight nose. Benteen was an extremely active man, and was physically powerful, despite his aged appearance.

Lieutenant Colonel Custer however, was heavily involved in the plethora of responsibilities of extricating the 7th Cavalry from the village of Chief Black Kettle. The successful counterattack by his mounted cavalry on the attack force of Indians had temporarily opened an avenue for escape.

"There's no time for it, Benteen," replied Custer tersely, prompting Benteen to fling his fur cap to the snow.

Elliott was literally on his own.

Chapter Eleven: Brazen Naturism!

As the crow flies, buffeted in the frigid arctic blasts of freezing headwinds, the scene unfolding at the Washita River was two days from Fort Dodge, Kansas.

The pleasant, inviting smell of burnt hickory carried in the polar wind as the crow soared above the columns of gray smoke that curled hazily from chimneys of Fort Dodge. The wood-fueled smoke streams were then swept away in the arctic gusts into distant tree lines.

The aroma of hickory smoke mixed with the dripping fat of pork ribs, spitted rabbit, and raccoon. The alluring scent caused the nostrils of a painted face in one of the cathedrals of ice that defined the frozen forest to flare and scent the wind.

The warrior's face was smeared profusely with red, black, yellow and white war paint made of iron oxides, berries, crushed roots and beets. Hand prints painted in black charcoal mixed with buffalo fat and saliva were imprinted on either side of his visage. The shaved head on both flanks of the massive, swaying roach was painted a deep ocher, extending down the warrior's forehead before changing into a series of bold black and white horizontal slashes. The face was broad and angular, being well defined.

The brave was joined by others; first only a few, then hundreds, nostrils flared, scenting the succulent odors carried on the wind from Fort Dodge…

Distinct, and sometimes conflicting personalities dwelt within the confines of quarried granite of this fort. Fort Dodge was a critical way station on the Santa Fe Trail for the wagon trains bound for New Mexico.

On any given day within the officers' quarters, habits of routine, such as a brisk strut from the steaming sassafras scented bath to the bedroom would have been unremarkable.

Under normal circumstances a young woman's ablutions may have been performed without a second thought and perchance bereft any premeditation at all. However, the circumstances that prevailed within the Custer household seldom could be categorized as normal.

Boredom forthwith set in among the house bound women, and within the Custer housing unit Eliza busied herself, humming enthusiastically in the kitchen while Margaret and Beverly talked.

"Now is a consummate opportunity!" Libbie thought.

"While they are happily engrossed in their dialogue amongst each other, I can feign to be so absorbed in my own matters that I disremembered my bath robe. They will be compelled to look, although they will certainly pretend not to." Elizabeth ruminated the bold scheme. She repeated it to herself over and over, playing it out in her mind. She was rehearsing.

Libbie contemplated the interesting concept for several minutes more; minutes that seemed to stretch interminably. She felt the suppressed excitement well up. She longed for those fleeting times of youth, spent in the dressing room, before and after gymnasium.

Elizabeth Bacon Custer made her fantasy become reality and walked barefoot from the bathroom quickly, pretending to be absorbed in drying her hair with the towel as she padded past her talking friends. Then, seeing that the door to Eliza's room was wide open - she made the spontaneous decision to enter that room instead, because it faced adjacent to the women who had pretended not to notice her.

However, Beverly had of late been made uncomfortable by Elizabeth Custer's occasional "nonchalant" episodes of naturism.

The brazen act of openness went unnoticed by Eliza, who hummed a religious hymn as she chopped carrots, potatoes, onions and prepared a large opossum for the oven.

The marsupial, dressed out and sloppy with fat, had been bathed in honey prior to stuffing its body cavity with sweet potatoes, salted butter, bay leaves, chive and chicory. These things Eliza did lovingly before putting it within a broiler and into the oven. The opossum would seethe in its own globules of fat and the sapidity of the tender, succulent meat would surpass that of even the finest pot roast. The juicy meat would literally melt in the mouth.

Beverly felt constrained and even more vexed by the way she saw Margaret's eyes follow the dimpled, jiggling derrière of her sister in law.

Margie continued speaking to Beverly, even though her attention was directed to the servant's room, where Libbie toweled her wet hair – she had not even closed the door behind her.

Beverly and Margaret continued their moronic conversation which pertained to an unmarried school teacher, around whom there circulated sordid speculations. Malicious, aberrant rumors threatened to ruin the attractive, middle-aged woman's career.

The over-qualified teacher was employed in the fort's second-rate school and was far beneath her qualifications. If she had been a man, a faculty position at one of the nation's top universities would have been appropriate. Had there been an all-female academic institution with a demanding position available, that also would have suited her more than the far flung, remote frontier school.

"I can find no fault with the woman," stated Beverly matter of factly, she continued her defense of the teacher, whom she would pass on the main street of

Fort Dodge occasionally and speak with in the sutler store. It irritated Beverly that the adult women all seemed to loath and distance themselves from the school marm.

"People can be so cruel," continued Beverly, "So what if she is thirty-five years old and has never been married nor seen with a man!" exclaimed Beverly.

"I heard that one of the boys in her English class – a red headed bully with freckles had placed a thumb tack on her chair," replied Margaret. She leaned back into the comfortable couch and ran her right hand through her hair as she spoke.

"The teacher," continued Margaret, "came back into the room and had sat down heavily onto the thumbtack prior to grading tests. There was a delayed reaction in which the class thought that the tack had fallen to the floor – but no!

"After a space of about a full minute the woman sprang to her feet, aghast and screaming in pain and shock! The class was beside themselves in laughter – such unseemly mirth!

"The distraught teacher, losing her composure demanded through tears and broken voice to know who had placed the tack onto her chair. She demanded to know! Even as she removed the pushpin from her tender behind. The poor woman fled the class room, weeping!"

"It's awful, the way the townspeople are treating that poor woman," Beverly agreed. She sincerely felt sympathy for the woman.

"It is the fear – the misunderstanding," replied Margaret.

"Men always seek to undermine the independence of women," explained Margaret who continued, adding, "and a woman who does not become a slave to a hideous male-beast is ostracized and often times ruined.

"I dread the day when my brother forces me to marry one of his friends. George Armstrong will force me to, of course. He will thrust a man upon me to further his career. I just hate to contemplate it."

Beverly saw Margaret continuing to observe Elizabeth in a frank, admiring way.

Libbie stood in front of the large mirror, mounted upon an old Victorian dresser hand carved from black walnut. The five-foot four inches, twenty-six-year-old was brushing her lustrous auburn hair with long, powerful strokes while she watched her reflection in the cracked, tarnished mirror.

The dresser, which had seen better days, consisted of four drawers only. However, the massive mirror that was affixed to it was nearly double the dresser's height, elevating the article of bedroom furniture, as a whole, to almost eight feet.

"These irascible tangles," Libbie complained to her audience, without looking at them (she could see them in the mirror), "are sufficient to drive a woman as mad as a hatter!"

Each tangle and snag accentuated the impetus of every brush stroke, culminating in the genesis of an utter display of quivering, bosom ecstasy.

Beverly was absentmindedly ignoring Margaret's commendations which were laudatory to the spinster schoolmarm and in the main deleterious to all men. This derision was not limited to adult men but digressed to boys and the male gender of all the animal kingdom as well.

The days after the circus had left Fort Dodge, the Norther had once more forced the women to become housebound. Beverly had become annoyed at Libbie's redundant absence of modesty; she felt that the behavior was inappropriate, and it irritated her that Libbie did not pull the door shut.

The dark-haired woman's tongue struck at Margaret like a poker in the hands of a widow. "I'm not much surprised at the boldness of Libbie, which I have seen in other women before. But the crude and unabashed way in which you clearly seem to enjoy observing your sister in law uncovered makes me feel very uncomfortable," Beverly said to Margaret, averting her gaze temporarily from Margaret and accidentally getting a full, head on view of Libbie's pursuance.

"How dare you!" expostulated Margaret at the demeaning accusation. "You would be prudent to remember under whose roof you abide!" threatened Margaret.

"Well, it's making me uncomfortable," countered the brunette, feeling her pulse rise.

"It's your loss if you can't appreciate beauty incarnate," riposted Margie, edging more closely to Beverly, she was biting her lower lip, then more softly she added, "it's going to be a woman's world, and the sooner you realize that the better things will become for you."

Margaret's eyes surveyed Beverly's jet-black hair, spun back tightly into a bun behind a crown on which the brow was symmetrical with high set, pleasantly perceptible cheek bones. The forehead was unlined, and the eyebrows plucked into wisps onto which liner had been applied. Enigmatic eyes, the color of black agate were set neither too far apart nor too close together. The nose was small, and the mouth petite and cruel. The chin was delicate, and the jaw strongly set. Overall, the face was one of peculiar beauty – almost like those seen in the paintings of the harems of Persian satraps.

Margaret's anger was tempered by the good looks of the woman, and she felt perplexed at the excitement invoked by the angry way in which the strange female had spoken to her.

Margie tried to imagine how Beverly would appear if she became truly angry with her. Margaret made herself see, for a split second, Beverly shouting at her, cursing and invoking epithets of profanity toward her.

"Were it not for the blizzard raging outside, I would take leave for a breath of fresh air," replied Beverly, her tone becoming subdued.

"These officers' quarters impart a sense of restriction – of being hemmed in. I spoke words born of frustration at what to me seems a confinement born of the weather. I meant nothing by them," Beverly explained, realizing the danger she had placed herself in; for she was totally indebted to the Custer women for her every need.

"Miss Libbie!" shouted the flabbergasted Eliza, the hem of her gray work dress swished about her hard-soled shoes known as "brogans," which clopped loudly as she ran. Eliza rushed across the spotlessly clean hardwood floor to assist her matron.

"Why you po' lil naked thang! Brushing yo' hair in a servant's room! With a servant's hair brush – oh! Po' Miss Libbie! Just hang in there 'till I get you some warm clothes from the upstairs!" pleaded Eliza. The earthiness and sincerity in the tone of Eliza's voice never failed to impress Libbie.

Eliza Brown had only four years before been an escaped slave from some estate in Virginia. The enigmatic woman had never regretted "adopting" the newly wed Custers in 1864.

She had cooked for them, did their laundry, and ran the household wherever the Army sent them. Eliza was a capable multitasker; skilled in all manners of assisting the almost helpless white woman. Whether it be in up to date military housing or army field tents.

Eliza cherished the Custers, catering to and pampering Elizabeth Custer unconsciously as though she were a priceless doll. She especially loved the eloquent, verbal prose that Libbie liked to hear herself impress people with.

"Oh, I'm just fine, Eliza. I will not ascend the stairway to my upstairs habitation, until I subdue these obstinate tangles! My hair! A Gordian Knot! Were I Alexander the Great I would cleave it!" exclaimed Libbie.

"Miss Libbie, I'm not sure what you talkin' about. But what we gonna do about cho' nakedness, Honey Child? You gonna get the pneumonia! Let me get you a nice evenin' dinner dress!" exclaimed Eliza, she was not putting on airs; she genuinely cared for the peculiar white woman.

Deep down Eliza felt that there was something not right with Libbie Custer, although she felt that it had a lot to do with the fact that Libbie had never known her mother. However, it gave Eliza a sense of satisfaction that she could earn such affection from people that she cherished. Elizabeth Custer possibly had a lot more wrong with her than simply needing a mother at this stage of her life, thought Eliza. But the Negress was not bothered too much by the idiosyncrasies of white women, who, she knew could be vicious – especially when it came to each other.

"You know, Eliza, I've told you once before that I never knew my mother at all," responded Libbie to Eliza's reassurances of procuring a wardrobe. Libbie was choosing her words carefully, watching the sensual lines of her lips move in the reflection of the mirror as she spoke. "Before I saw thirteen winters of age, my poor daddy was left with naught but my worthless self. My mother, along with my pitiable siblings, had all passed on their way to the Good Lord.

"My distraught father and my wretched self were to reside within a purgatory of loneliness, relieved only by the frequent hangings that my father applied to the vile miscreants that flourished within his jurisdiction." Libbie paused, collecting her thoughts and then continued.

"He would incarcerate them in penal institutions until my return from boarding school during the summer recess," Libbie ceased once more in her monologue and smiling, added, "then he would hang them while I watched."

"I know, Miss Libbie, I was there, with you," answered Eliza. "You an' the judge sho' liked dem hangins!" continued Eliza, smiling and involuntarily casting her gaze down as she fondly remembered Libbie's father, the old Judge Bacon.

Eliza stood at about the same height as Elizabeth and despite being whip thin, was heavily breasted. These were pulled in by the tightly buttoned, gray faded work dress. Eliza noticed one of the peculiarities of white women as she looked down, seeing that Elizabeth was dearth of a triangular thatch.

"My banal, day to day continuance has ever since been brightened with the most intense effulgence from that day outside the Sibley tent, when you adopted the General and myself into your caring bosom," Libbie said in a soft voice, turning to face Eliza and placing her hands on her servant's shoulders.

"I have come to love you as I would my mother," continued Libbie.

"I can vaguely recall her as one sees shadows in the lateness of the day, but I never knew her. You *are* my mother, Eliza." said Libbie softly. She smiled kindly as she spoke – like an angel, thought Eliza.

Eliza stood as though frozen, her hair was concealed by a turban of checkered cloth. Her forehead was broad, but not pronounced, and the intercanthal distance between her slate eyes was barely pronounced. Her cheek bones were broad, though, and conveyed the aspect of a heart shape to the contours of her face, shiny with bee's wax and corn oil. The jaw was not strongly set, and along with a diminutive chin, exaggerated the size of her lips. Eliza was very darkly pigmented; there being no suggestion of pedigree outside of African ancestry.

This was not the first time that white women had exhibited displays of endearment toward Eliza. It was akin to the way a girl sees a caring figurehead in her mother, thought the maid servant. Eliza was

154

aware of Elizabeth's emotional dependence on her, but the frank confession coming as it did, had caught the indomitable former slave off balance.

"I'm getting' you somethin' to put on, Miss Libbie," said Eliza, "so dat you don't come down with the pneumonia," she said the words haltingly, and wished to hurry from the room.

Eliza was rocked with emotions that she had only experienced once before; that also was a time when Libbie had compared her to her mother.

Never once in all of her life had Eliza cried, or experienced the sensation of her eyes tearing. Eliza was no stranger to the explosive emotional displays at the religious sermons, funerals and daily life of the completely segregated black community. But there was something behind the bright smile of Eliza which the long, straight snuff stained teeth concealed. The good humor, affability, and the convivial demeanor; they were all a subterfuge.

Inside the woman's head was an intense complexity of thought and beneath her chest pumped a cold heart. She was incapable of sentimental feelings, of emotions, or so she thought.

Eliza struggled with all of her innate strength to hold back her tears as she smiled, shook her head and frantically tried to mask the emotions that she could not much longer hold in abeyance.

When Eliza thought she could exit the room, Libbie began speaking again, compelling her to stay, for to exit while her matron spoke would be taken wrongly, and considered rude.

"I lament that it was one of my innumerable foibles that provoked this intrusion into your personal space; I have trespassed into the privacy of your own sanctuary, Eliza," apologized Libbie Custer.

"I'm fleeing to get you some clothes, Miss Libbie!" choked Eliza, hurrying toward the door.

"Momma?" whispered Libbie, "Momma? Don't go, don't leave me momma..."

Eliza froze, looking toward an imaginary point on the ceiling, as her lips trembled, and tears ran freely down her cheeks.

"But I could not bear," Libbie had said to Margaret after Eliza had left the room, "not for one moment more, that my unruly mane of hair be so unkempt as to put to shame my poor husband, who at this very moment could find himself facing those unwashed savages in a winter holocaust!"

It would be difficult for Elizabeth Custer to fathom the predicament that her soldier husband – a living legend, had put himself and his command into.

Nor could she have had an inkling of the fate of Major Elliott, who she openly despised on account that he had formerly commanded the 7th Cavalry. Elliott was seen by her as a possible threat to the command position of her husband.

Libbie's female intuition was uncanny; man-hater though she may have been, she keenly desired that her husband succeed professionally.

Secretly, within certain circles of powerful men, Libbie knew, there was a desire to see her husband accede as President of the United States. To her that would mean becoming the nation's First Lady – the most powerful woman on the earth. The threat that Major Elliott presented was never far from Libbie's mind.

Elliott had not wanted to relinquish command to Custer and had done so reluctantly. That Major Elliott would soon be abandoned without any attempt at rescue would have delighted Libbie. Such a way of removing a threat was right out of the Custers' play book.

Hurriedly, Eliza sought clothing from Libbie's upstairs room. For the moment though, Elizabeth Custer blocked all extraneous thoughts of the menacing specter of Major Elliott from her mind. She continued gazing upon the reflection of her natural state in the mirror.

Meanwhile, an ice world away deep in the Oklahoma Indian Territory, events would disprove one of Eliza's many verbose reassurances to Elizabeth of the general's control of the "Injuns." The situation was far from under control.

Chapter Twelve: Pursuit!

The tracks were not laid out in a single column, as experienced trackers would have made them in the knee-deep snow. Instead, there were multiple trails made individually; made in haste by Major Elliott's troop in chase of the dozen or so Cheyenne women and children.

The pursuing cavalrymen gave no thought to the energy they expended wastefully by the cutting of individual paths through the icy precipitate.

The separate paths made by Major Elliott's men seemed to go on interminably, leading further and further into a Nordic wasteland of icebound landscapes, in which massive oak trees ruptured and split – sounding like claps of thunder as the report carried through the icy valleys and snow clad, rolling hills.

Even miles away, the crack of massive tree limbs crashing to the frozen earth resonated heavily through the icy air, carried by the arctic wind out of the north and sounding like the dynamite of Chinese railway gangs.

Oddly, the sound of gunfire and the neighing of wounded horses seemed distant and detached, thought Major Elliott, his breath issuing in fetid steam as he panted from the exertion.

"Did you see that little filly back there?" Sergeant Major Walter Kennedy queried to Major Joel H. Elliott as he fought to stay up with the demanding pace set by the major, hoping desperately that they would stop for a break.

"You mean the good looking one that they said got the hots for Custer, when she saw him kill her father?" Elliott responded, adding, "There's another time and another place for that kind of talk. We've gotta bag these prisoners."

Major Elliott didn't like Sergeant Major Kennedy, in fact, neither did a lot of the men. The Army ranks were filled with immigrants, misfits, people who couldn't make it as civilians, and former Confederate soldiers.

The black haired, grey eyed, 160-pound Kennedy, standing at five feet, nine inches tall had been a Confederate lieutenant in the recent Civil War. Ever the opportunist, when the war ended Kennedy had signed up with the Union Army.

Known for being a backstabber who had quickly made it to the top of the enlisted ranks, few people trusted the dime dropping, two-faced boot licker and sycophant.

Wearing a pencil moustache and a goatee, the sergeant major was nevertheless a survivor, taking multiple bullet wounds when he was a rebel, and he could be a ruthless, cunning opponent.

Even the officers feared him, because of his keen knowledge of military regulations and whispered relationships with certain of the higher-ranking officers, some of them unmarried career soldiers, as was he.

"I'd do her anyplace, anytime," confided the good looking, recruiting poster image-like sergeant major.

Major Elliott raised his left arm, his hand forming a fist as they entered a shattered copse of frozen, disfigured, leafless trees, signaling for the party to halt. When giving hand arm signals, the major liked to use his left, keeping his gun hand free.

"She does inspire the better part of me," Elliott agreed with the sergeant major, adding, "we'll take ten right here."

"She's a raving beauty," Sergeant Major Kennedy said to himself, sitting atop a fallen tree and removing his boots, rubbing circulation into the cold, numb toes and feet through the regulation wool socks.

The enlisted men were battle seasoned and had spread into a semi-circle, facing outboard. They had to raise their voices to be heard over the wind,

Kennedy absent mindedly observed. He didn't really pay too much attention because he was more concerned by the blackened discoloration of his toes, which implied severe frost bite. If he didn't get medical attention soon, he knew, he would lose his toes.

Sergeant Major Kennedy observed also, through the thick curtain of falling snow, that Major Elliott had distanced himself from him and was gesticulating rapidly with Corporal William Carrick - regarding a topic of contention.

The sergeant major saw Major Elliott whip out his compass and shoot an azimuth in the direction of their march. Turning about face, the Major next took another compass reading. Then the major shouted above the wind to Corporal Carrick, who shook his head emphatically in the negative at what Elliott seemed to want to do.

It had begun thundering again, in a rare phenomenon known as thunder snow. The snow as a result came down more heavily, in thick cottony clumps – threatening to cover their tracks.

Major Elliott studied the troubling tracks that the lanky, smart mouthed Corporal Carrick pointed out. The spoor of the interlopers was huge – bigger than any foot tracks he had ever seen. The five feet six-inch corporal placed his booted foot into one of the tracks; the track easily surpassed his foot size by two times.

The tracks differed from the boot prints and moccasin prints that preceded them in that they splayed out of proportion to the length. But it was particularly worrisome that the large footprints were clearly in pursuit of the Cheyenne.

Then Elliott looked over at Kennedy, who he saw sitting on the fallen tree, rubbing his feet. Kennedy was looking right back at him.

"I gotta get that snitch outa here, somehow," ruminated Elliott to Corporal Carrick, "he'll rat me out to the Boy General the first chance he gets, if he sees me let my men have some fun with the prisoners – if we can ever catch up with them!"

"HEEEEYAAAAAAAAAAAAAAAAAHHHHHHH!!!!!!!!!" a scream materialized from swirling mists of snow nearby. It was not the scream of a warrior who attacks, but rather, the scream of a man in extreme agony.

"Fall into a column! Carrick, pick someone you think is expendable, and put him on point! Sergeant Major Kennedy, you stick close to me. *Now let's head'em dead'em over there!"* ordered the revitalized Civil War hero.

Elliott had been, it was well known, shot through both lungs and left for dead at the Battle of White's Station, while under the command of the now Captain Benteen.

Later, Elliott had been appointed as a sort of ad-hoc or acting regimental commander and had accompanied Colonel Grierson in his famous raid through Mississippi.

Major Elliott had seen his star rise with the Civil War and was one of the fortunate few who had seen it continue to rise with the end of hostilities.

Sergeant Major Kennedy was pulling his cold stiffened boots back on when again the blood curdling scream manifested itself carrying on the icy wind through the ice castles of frozen trees and snowy gulches. It seemed to come from the direction in which they were headed, but Kennedy could not be sure.

"I think it's coming from up ahead!" shouted Elliott.

Above Kennedy and Elliott, thick, gun metal grey nimbostratus clouds scudded along at one thousand feet, headed to the south, thrust along on by the bleak polar wind.

The low-level clouds urged the snow flurries into a hoary, swirling vortex of pallidity. Small funnel shaped phenomena known as "snow devils" skipped and danced their way frenetically over the icy terrain. The impetus of the snow devils seemed to be encouraged by what sounded like the shrieking of Valkyries through the denuded trees.

The major, corporal, sergeant major along with fifteen other soldiers walked in a single file, with rifles facing outboard into a confined rectangular frozen area.

The area was cleared and seemed to have been used as a primitive camp site. It was obvious that they had entered a rudimentary, no frills hunting camp that had been erected with only a single purpose in mind.

The bodies of thirty Cheyenne warriors hung suspended from tree branches, bereft of clothing and upside down. They had been trussed and hoisted up while not yet dead, apparently - at least some of them.

Without exception they were eviscerated from the peritoneal area to the sternum. The discards had been collected and heaped unceremoniously into a large visceral mound, already frozen in a convoluted heap.

Of the fleeing women and children there were few signs, but piles of clothing lay strewn about the Spartan hunting camp, partially covered in the mounting inches of fresh snow. Quickly the men donned the extra clothing, heedless of the freezing gore that spattered the heavy winter coats.

One of the soldiers, named Private Thomas Christie, brought up a shivering Cheyenne woman and several small children under the age of ten.

"Sir! These are all we could find, they had been captured and were probably going to be dressed out like those poor devils!" said Private Christie.

"Cheyenne don't do this," mumbled the worried Major Elliott to Christie, turning to see the prisoners as a gust of wind blew a large clump of snow from a tree limb, knocking his badger fur hat from his head and causing him to utter an explicative.

"Cheyenne don't skin each other alive, either – this was done by someone else," added Kennedy, who wanted more than anything to be gone from the campsite, "anyway, this place gives me the creeps!"

"What do you infer from these malicious atrocities?" Major Elliott asked Sergeant Major Kennedy, then he added his own speculations as an afterthought, "Apache maybe? Tribal warfare?"

"I don't know," answered Kennedy, brushing the snow from the buffalo fur coat he'd picked up from the site of the butchery, "but these prisoners would answer the riddle, if one among us could but speak their tongue."

"Sergeant Major," exclaimed cold-numbed Major Elliott, keeping his voice down, "I am of a mind that this diabolical mystery in some way ties in with the glowing orb that we saw this morning."

Although it seemed to him that his group was alone with the corpses, there was a nagging doubt in his mind He wished he could deny the reality of the situation. He felt as though they were being watched. In fact, his sixth sense warned him so strongly *that he was certain of it!*

The light, frigid breeze had transformed itself again into a bone cracking, icy gust of gale force, howling hellishly out of the north and compelling all of the corpses to swing and oscillate, eerily careening into one another.

The cordage emitted sustained rubbing sounds that occasionally squeaked as the rawhide dug its way into the ice of the frozen branches and rubbed against the wood.

"Get these loathsome prisoners out of here," exclaimed Major Elliott, his words carried the tone of one who has had an inspiration, "and back to where they can be interrogated!"

"Yes Sir! I'll run them back to the village and I'll give Custer heads up on the situation here," stated Kennedy, "and our interpreters can interrogate these prisoners and find out who is going around butchering these people!"

"Yeah, go ahead and do that. Head back to the village with them," ordered Major Elliott, relieved to be rid of the distrusted non-commissioned officer.

Elliott regarded the peculiar, Cupid faced sergeant major enigmatically for a moment before the howling of an enormous pack of wolves caused him to turn his head suddenly in their direction.

It was then that Kennedy stepped off toward the village, having his captives lead the way with their hands tied in front of them. They had not traversed 100 feet before they were ensconced in the swirling white mists of snow.

Major Elliott was confronted with indecision as his mind raced against the devil to deduce the next move – whether or not to continue the search. To keep hunting for the elusive fugitives, while the perpetrators of the atrocities were probably nearby defied common sense.

"Fall in!" shouted the major, prompting the soldiers to fall loosely into ranks, facing him, at the position of semi-attention.

"Listen up! We are heading back to the Cheyenne village! We're giving up the search for prisoners! Tighten up your gear and let's get out of here!" ordered Major Elliott.

The order was met with shouts of relief from the band of cavalrymen and they headed in the direction of Black Kettle's village toward the sound of gunfire. The group encountered large snow drifts impeding their progress. The drifts of snow resembled gigantic, bleached ocean waves as they heaped up like sand dunes on any obstacle in their path.

It occurred during the incessant fury of the blizzard that a discernable shape materialized gradually into view, like some dimly seen form in a nightmare that is at once familiar, but at the same time not recognizable.

At first it was barely distinguishable from the other snow-covered features, but it revealed itself to be the body of a man – a white man – minus its integumentary sheathing.

There was no indication of sentience emanating from within the unclothed body, neither was there an indication of life. The cadaver was strung suspended upside down, skinned and eviscerated like the others.

Who the carcass had been was open to conjecture, as it spun in a winding motion on its tether until fully wound and unspun menacingly on the rawhide cord in the rimy caressing of the arctic wind.

A blast of polar air swung the cadaver violently about, facing the approaching group of soldiers. These were soldiers who now thought only of survival from the elements. Whoever the sinister appearing cadaver had been didn't rank highly on the ledger of their priorities.

The twenty-eight-year-old major approached the apparition and then stepped around the back of the dangling corpse, which was suspended by its ankles. Motioning his men to come closer he then stepped to the front of it shouting, "Listen up! It is Sergeant Major Kennedy! He's been butchered out like a steer! Whoever did this is nearby – watching us! Secure your gear and make sure your carbines are loaded up! Get ready to move out of here at a route march!

"We might make it back to the command before total darkness, but we are going to have to move out in the open and quickly, sacrificing caution! We are being hunted - and we are *getting out of here!*"

Chapter Thirteen: Run!!!

The dangling, upside down Kennedy looked on; on into eternity with his almost prescient, lifelike stare as the dark figures of his fellow troopers milled all around him, tightening straps and securing gear prior to departing at a route march – a march that is familiar to all soldiers. A route march is a march at a rapid pace that is almost at a full run.

Major Elliott kneeled in front of Sergeant Major Kennedy, seeing into the distance of Kennedy's grey eyes, searching for words to say, wanting to apologize for having to leave him hanging like this.

Elliott saw himself growing smaller and smaller in the reflection of Kennedy's eyes – then suddenly Kennedy's eyes came alive and locked fiercely on his own!

"Don't leave me here! *DON'T LEAVE ME LIKE THIS!*" growled the upside-down Sergeant Major Kennedy, who grabbed Major Elliott around the waist in a bear hug of inhuman strength.

"Oh, my Lord!" shouted Elliott, "Soldiers! To me men! *I AM BESET!!!*"

The major reflexively tried to career backwards to break the sergeant major's iron grasp. But the rawhide cord simply allowed the disemboweled man to swing forward, not releasing Major Elliott.

Major Elliott had panicked and was shouting for help; help which was not forthcoming. Elliott's commands were obeyed with silence instead of action. The troop of the horrified enlisted men watched in stupefied, superstitious terror at the grotesque struggle unfolding before them.

"I TOLD YOU TO GET OVER HERE AND HELP ME!!!" screamed Elliott at the top of his lungs. He was leaning back at a forty-five-degree angle, trying to break the growling Vitruvian Man's bear hug.

Elliott's tendons stood out on the sides of his thick neck like steel cables as he strained to break free, screaming, *"SOMEBODY HELP ME!!!"*

The troop was composed of soldiers of vastly differing sociological backgrounds. The ethnically diverse group of soldiers acted independently and resented one another to varying degrees, often bordering hatred. But at this moment unit cohesion was intact and the soldiers reacted as a single entity; not assisting their officer in charge.

Looking at his charges Elliott said, *"Don't y'all run! DON'T Y'ALL DARE RUN!!!"*

170

Sergeant Major Kennedy pulled Major Elliott in closer to him, growling, *"YOU CAN'T LEAVE ME HANGIN' LIKE THIS!!!"*

"Run!" shouted Carrick, "Make for the village!"

The troop, minus Major Elliott was now led by Corporal Carrick, who was in de facto command. They had set off at an all-out run, rather than a more energy efficient route march. They headed in the direction of the gunfire emanating from Black Kettle's village.

When they were out of sight of Kennedy and Elliott the group halted on Carrick's order, so that he could take a compass reading and confirm their bearings.

"Make for that knoll that stands above the treeline!" ordered the assertive corporal, made aggressive in his determination to make it back with his men to the main body of the 7th Cavalry.

A red dot, cast by a weapon's laser sight appeared on the back of one of the soldiers. Then there was the sound of a very loud, nearby gunshot. The cavalryman collapsed to his knees and fell forward as much from the impact as from the sudden drop in blood pressure.

Rather than attempt to remain standing and deduce who it was that had fired the projectile that had struck the cavalryman, Carrick reacted instinctively.

"Make a 360!" shouted the corporal, intending to form a circular defensive position, with weapons facing outboard.

"What about him?!" shouted one of the privates, referring to their mortally wounded fellow soldier.

"Never mind him! Make a 360 and get those weapons facing outboard!" commanded Corporal Carrick, shouting as loud as he could to be heard above the wind.

"What?!" Carrick thought, seeing the stocky figure of the dead private being lifted and hurried away by an individual of huge stature. The interloper had infiltrated the group surreptitiously. It had an enormous human form, but only the murderer's back was visible to Corporal Carrick as it hurried away with its prize.

Carrick watched, as though trying to ascertain that what he was witnessing in the blinding blizzard was real. The dead private had been stripped and hauled upside down by his ankles, where he hung, swinging from a rope slung over a tree branch. Then the huge killer turned to face the soldiers, about fifty yards away. The soldiers stared back at it. It was a stare down that lasted for about a minute.

"Shoot it! Shoot it to pieces – or it will kill us all!" the alarmed corporal shouted. Fearing that he could not be overheard in the wind, Corporal Carrick reiterated, *"BLOW THE THING TO PIECES! GET IT???"*

Shooting into the chest of the eight feet tall humanoid and knocking it off balance, some of the bullets thudded into the exposed soldier. The cavalryman was oblivious to the impacts as he hung unnaturally, suspended by his ankles from the frozen tree branch.

"It has to be one of the hunters. Maybe a forward scout, a tracker - ahead of the others, and detached from the main hunting party," said Corporal Mercer to Carrick.

"There was a main group that had been trailing the fleeing Cheyenne, and now it's on our trail," answered Corporal Carrick.

The massive, man-like form sprang to its feet, growling like a large, wounded ape, and faced off against the soldiers. This time it raised a large caliber, semiautomatic pistol. Before it could get off another trigger squeeze, the high capacity weapon was shot from its six-fingered hand. The weapon flew twenty feet and was buried in the snow.

The impact of multiple large caliber bullets caused the hunter to reel backwards against the snow-covered tree, inducing the loose snow to spill upon it. For a moment the snow covered it and obscured the immense human-like form. Ocher red blood spilled from a half dozen entry and exit wounds.

The hunter, for lack of a better definition, sprang to its feet and ran hollering like a mad man into the frozen, penumbral tree line. Even after it had vanished into the icy woods the maddened hollering persisted veering off in its direction as it ran.

The men had faced difficulty reloading their Spencer Model 1860 carbines. Their numbed fingers lacked the sensation to correctly enter the bullets through the tube in the butt stock of the weapons. Some of the bullets fell, vanishing several inches into the softer surface snow that blanketed the frozen, deeper snow in a fluffy, alabaster quilt.

Despite the fact that it was a black powder, 19th Century weapon, it was magazine fed and lever operated. This allowed for rapid firing of a .52 caliber bullet, weighing over an ounce. The hammer had to be cocked manually each time the carbine was fired, and the copper, rim fired cartridge ejected. Anything taking a hit from one of these projectiles would sustain a grievous injury.

The Spencer had a seven-round tubular magazine and a maximum effective range of 500 yards. Despite opinions to the contrary, men with good eyesight often exceeded the carbine's maximum effective range.

"Run!" shouted Corporal Carrick at the top of his voice.

"What direction?" responded several of the bewildered men.

"In the direction of Custer's gunfire! Head for the village!" answered Carrick as his ability to perform as a noncommissioned officer was tested in the demanding situation.

"HEEEYAHHHHHHHHHHHHHHHH!!!" came a blood curdling yell from several hundred yards away, behind them, from the direction they had come.

"It's Major Elliott!" shouted one of the men.

"He's being dressed out alive – now let's run for it!" shouted Carrick in response.

"No! We've got to go back and help him!" shouted Corporal Mercer.

"Hell! What are you waiting for? *You* go back there then! As for the rest of us, let's stick together and try to find our way back to the village!" riposted Corporal Carrick, determined to get his team back to the Custer element.

To the direct front indistinctly visible in the swirling curtain of snow was a vaguely discernable treeline of ice shattered white oak, of which the heavy burden of massive icicles had made the cyclopean branches snap and break like the bones of an old man falling from his bed. Within this was a lair in which lay dying a solitary figure, like a wounded lion.

Were it not for the heavy rise and fall of the blood-stained chest in the freezing, open area of the small clearing, the human-like form, dressed as it was could have remained totally unseen.

The humanoid was wearing a silvery white jumpsuit akin to a pair of coveralls. Over the clothing was a utility belt sustained by suspenders onto which the holster of a weapon depended, along with various other accoutrements. The thin clothing was out of place for the setting and seemed to offer no warmth whatsoever.

The head was large but in proportion to the eight-foot length of the body. The pate was destitute of hair, as was the humanoid countenance, which bore the semblance of Caucasian features. The eyes, closely set together, were black as inkwells. The ears were large and conspicuous in proportion to the head. The skull was oblong to the point of appearing dicephalic, and were it not for the nose, imparted a Cro-Magnon-like visage. The nose was long and straight, the nostrils flared as it tried to breath. Overlarge veins stood out, pulsating faintly on the sides of the temples. Arching its spinal column, it dug the back of its head into the snow and shouted in distinct, unintelligible words. It seemed to Carrick that it was shouting a plea for assistance – but he could not be sure.

The voice was baritone and had the resonance like that of a large man made barrel chested from a lifetime of smoking. The sound was answered in kind, the orators ensconced far behind the sheets of falling snow, where Elliott and Kennedy had been.

More sounds akin to those made by the largest males of the human species called out from another direction in the unrecognizable baritone language. The shouts originated far back within the thick concealment of trees.

"More than one group," said Carrick.

"It's like a big game hunt, and we are the trophies!" exclaimed Mercer.

Other figures began to arrive, announced by their indecipherable speech and the snapping of frozen undergrowth. They were visible at first only by their broad shoulders twisting and stooping as they pushed their way through the frozen tree branches and saplings. Then they appeared suddenly in full view before kneeling down beside their fallen companion.

"Let them have it!" ordered Corporal Carrick as his soldiers broke the 360 and formed a firing line to either side of him. They let loose a volley, knocking all four of the silver suited figures down.

The giants quickly recovered, running a short way zig zagging, then dropping and rolling in the snow, skillfully throwing off the aim of the marksmen. They were seeking cover and attempting to dodge the gunfire. Once at the tree line, they regained their feet and ran back into the frozen timber, shouting unintelligibly. One of them staggered and fell when he was hit again; he did not get up a second time.

'Who are they?" asked several of the soldiers.

"Not Cheyenne. Cheyenne are big, *but not that big!*" answered one of the men in the group.

"I don't know, but they've got to have a camp around here somewhere, and we better find it or else we'll freeze!" answered Carrick.

"Aren't we going back to where the rest of the 7th Cavalry is?" asked Mercer, confused and desperate.

"No," answered Carrick, "too late for that now! We'd never make it! Let's follow their tracks!" ordered the corporal.

"Found them over here – a bunch of them!" shouted one of the cavalrymen.

The dwindling band of soldiers went as a single file group, following the foot prints which led to a large clearing of melted snow and ice. A huge, flat saucer shaped object rested on four gigantic hydraulic struts, in an enormous area where the trees had been ripped aside and everything had been flattened out.

An opening was visible on the underside of the massive object, from which a ramp rested on the bare, incinerated ground that had received such a blast of heat as to turn the surface to glass.

The 1,600 feet in diameter, saucer shaped, gray disk was substantially thicker in its center, having an ovate, proportional center mass that averaged 200 feet, from bottom to top.

There were dozens of flashing strobe lights, of various hues both above and beneath the craft. These winked on, then faded in brightness before illuminating to full intensity again. Smaller, brighter lights blinked off and on incandescently around the entire rim of the dun colored disc.

The soldiers approached bravely, like riflemen and without fear. They looked from left to right, crouching, with carbines at the ready. They approached with the fatalism gained through the experience of firefights.

Hand and arm signals defeated the attempts of the wind to confound their intent of boarding the craft. The cavalrymen were determined to enter the disk and escape the elements.

"When we get in there – kill them! Save your questions. We are going in like this: *We go in and we go in shooting! Prepare to rush! NOW - RUSH!!!*" shouted Corporal Carrick.

Carrick and the other soldiers, including Corporal Mercer made it up the ramp and into the interior of the enormous space craft, which was washed in a soft red light.

The high pitched, deafening sound of hydraulics had initiated even before the infantry style rush. The craft began lifting the ramp in an attempt to deny entry to the extraneous threat. The gigantic hunters had now become the hunted.

Suddenly, from around a bulkhead, five of the eight-feet-tall crewmembers appeared and froze in place. They seemed surprised and hesitated momentarily. It was if they were unsure of their next move. They raised their arms, hands open in the universal sign of surrender.

"TARGETS DIRECT FRONT! shouted Carrick, adding, *"ENGAGE!!!"*

The hydraulic ramp of the saucer continued lifting up, accompanied by the heavy report of carbine fire within the enemy vessel.

When the ramp completed its journey and sealed the doorway closed, it cut off completely all sounds from within the craft.

A loud hum emanated from beneath the craft accompanied with a deafening explosion of exhaust.

The exhaust manifested itself in a hot blast of fire which sent steaming, melted snow, mud and debris in all directions. The vehicle's liquid fuel cryogenic engine initiated lift off, exerting a herculean 300,100,000 pounds of thrust.

The ground shook as though rocked by an earthquake surpassing 8.9 on the Richter scale. The soldiers left outside the vehicle fled from the fire ball and flying water from steaming, hissing melted snow and ice.

Within the tepid confines of the saucer however, warmed fingers hastily reloaded smoking, hot Spencer repeaters.

"TARGET RIGHT!!!" shouted Carrick, leaning forward into a crouch while pivoting to face an opening door that slid sideways. The soldiers were ejecting spent copper casings working the lever action of the Spencers to load another one into the chamber. Then

they cocked back the hammer again with a reassuring clicking sound. Those who already had a round in the tube let go with it.

Three colossal, human-like figures armed with assault rifles stood framed against the open doorway. They were bathed in an orange-red light which flooded in from behind them, washing them in a tangerine dream. They shifted reflexively and lifted their rifles in an attempt to go full auto from the hip. The cavalrymen fired first, and the leading two humanoids went down while the third one returned fire, staggering backwards and shooting wildly - hitting the door as it slid closed with a whishing sound.

Unknown to Corporal Carrick, he was leading his assault team to the ship's main server station, in which two seats were occupied by the humanoids. They composed part of the flight crew and were frantically operating complex control sticks. These were guidance controls that arose from the floor and were situated between their knees. On the control sticks were many buttons.

The pilot and copilot were seated in low slung cushioned chairs that were bolted into a severely confined space. Whether aware or not of the impending threat, the pilots did not abandon their station.

The bulkheads surrounding the cockpit were engulfed with control boards comprised of luminescent arrays of flickering lights. There were multiple electronic instrumentation panels with digital and analog displays in neon green, and controls consisting of buttons, switches and touch screens.

Cathode ray tubes provided optical screens for the pilots to view the outside of the saucer.

The soldiers comprehended at a fundamental level that they were aboard an extraterrestrial spacecraft. Not having time to think beyond the present, they had come upon another of the space craft's servos and shot it to pieces.

Over a hundred computers operated the software and more than two dozen computers served as backups. If one or more computers went offline, the others would compensate.

Carrick shot into one of the aerospace servo amplifiers, disabling the feedback transducers and throwing the servo actuators offline.

Yellow warning lights immediately illuminated, alerting the flight crew of impending disaster. Promptly one of the pilots began flipping body flap switches to compensate as the other computers raced to take over the offline computer. The cabin was momentarily blackened in the confined space as acrid spent black gunpowder smoke entered through the emergency ventilation system.

Away from the dual seated cockpit, the interior was larger than it appeared. The sound of gunfire was deafening within the tortuous, confined areas which the cavalrymen cleared as they advanced.

The electronic digital displays of what seemed to be numbers and hieroglyphical alphabet were barely perceptible through the gloom of the gun smoke that hung suspended in a dirty haze through the pulsating, eerie red light.

The automated annunciator matrix of the spacecraft's alarm system had become fully engaged, emitting an amplified, klaxon-like conglomeration of multiple alarms – at least three distinctly different alarms were clearly discernable.

Echoing above the bedlam of alarms a calm female computer generated voice spoke at timed intervals, issuing verbal warnings in an unfathomable language.

The soldiers, rid of their winter clothing, were dressed in blue cavalry uniforms. The yellow bandana scarves emblematic of US cavalry were around their necks. The scarves extended triangularly downward between their shoulder blades.

The ruthless appearing, unshaven cavalrymen provided a bizarre juxtaposition of past versus future. They were bathed in the violently flashing distress-strobe lights as they boldly advanced through the corridors at a crouch, firing from left to right.

The cavalrymen, led by Corporal Carrick, proceeded in a wedge formation protected on all sides – firing their weapons. They fired carefully at the furtive figures that darted for cover in the smoky, undulating twilight cast by the alarm strobes through the haze of gunsmoke.

Over the din of gunfire and deafening mix of alarms, the automated female voice continued to update warnings of the soldiers' position in her calm, tranquil voice. The cavalrymen advanced inexorably, boldly, like infantry.

The floor was abruptly tilted at a steep incline as the enormous flying disk acquired the angle needed prior to acceleration toward outer space. The acute angle caused the cavalrymen to stumble backward, into ruined electronic equipment that emitted sparks and dirty black electrical smoke.

Outside, some of the soldiers fired repeatedly on the departing saucer, as it was changing in hues from gray to copper, then to orange and red.

Corporal Carrick was suddenly thrown violently back against the bulkhead as an individual crewmember – armed with a deeply blued service automatic delivered multiple rounds of small caliber bullets. The tips of the projectiles were hollow, filled with explosive and capped with a polymer type ball. The projectiles struck Carrick where a red laser dot pinpointed the trajectory.

The remaining blue uniformed cavalrymen inside the saucer sought cover instinctively. They adjusted their balance by leaning into the bulkheads as the craft accelerated speed at an upward angle and dipped left, then right. The saucer shuddered violently as it fought the earth's gravitational pull prior to entering into low level orbit.

The enormous humanoid that had shot Corporal Carrick pressed the magazine release of the pistol with its thumb, causing a thin single stack magazine to drop to the deck.

Frantically, the crewmember sought another magazine with which to reload the weapon. Failing in its endeavor, it rushed the soldiers like an infantryman and fell to their obsolete, but effective black powder carbines.

When the herculean beings had departed the Washita River basin in their glowing, scintillating space craft they had been seen by thousands of the warriors who were rushing from other villages further up the Washita to assist Black Kettle and Little Rock. These warriors immediately took the craft under fire with their repeating arms. They cursed and invoked the names of their gods as they shook their emptied rifles at the fleeing object.

Within the confines of the saucer shaped craft, the desperate struggle was ensuing. But for the cavalrymen left behind on the snow-covered terrain, matters had taken a turn for the worse.

The soldiers who were left behind went to their revolvers rather than reload the carbines as the forest came alive with Indians. Some broke and ran toward the heavy oak trees that stood solemnly in the twilight with their shattered, ghostly branches, laden with icicles ten feet long and weighing hundreds of pounds each.

"Save the last bullet for yourself! Save the last bullet for yourself! *They are upon us!*" shouted one of the last remaining soldiers of the Elliott troop.

Aboard the low orbit saucer, the alien pilot and copilot worked patiently now at the controls within the cockpit. They were protected by two monstrous henchmen who had just arrived. These were the first individuals of a large immediate reaction force.

The main reaction force was of company strength and was rushing from the ship's armory, located deep within the bowels of the ship, armed with shoulder fired automatic weapons. They were led by shouting lieutenants whose commands were muted by a new alarm that originated from the deeper within the ship, sounding eerily like the warning call of a blue whale, but amplified to thundering volume.

The oscillating alarm strobe lights made the main reaction force appear as though they were running in slow motion, with their assault rifles held at the position of port arms. Atop their heads were helmets akin to those worn by the Germans in later wars and they were protected in body armor. Their utility belts bristled with extra ammunition.

The orders shouted from the open mouths of their lieutenants were muted by the blue whale calls, which began as though from far away and increased to deafening amplitude before dying off again.

The two towering members of the rapid response team who arrived to protect the pilots were coy to the appearance of the blue uniforms of the 7th Cavalry. They regarded the soldiers as dangerous pathogens.

Both xenomorphs were armed with shoulder strapped, open bolt, low slung submachine guns, which did not a have safety selector switch and could only be fired fully automatic.

The reaction team crouched and leaned forward as they began firing from the hip. Two disbursed streams of high velocity bullets, ball mixed with tracer, sped from the muzzles at 3,000 feet per second.

The muzzles of the weapons lifted with the recoil, raising the strike of the projectiles and spattering the metal bulkheads, throwing sparks and ricochets.

The metal jacketed bullets thoroughly perforated three soldiers, causing them to reflexively shoot wildly, and hit the pilot in his left temple. Another of the colossal beings went down to its knees breaking its fall with the folding stock of its empty submachinegun.

The remaining humanoid dropped a spent magazine to the metal floor of the craft, slapping another into the magazine well as the remaining cavalryman's revolver drove a round into the Goliath's left eye.

The co-pilot pulled himself laboriously from the low-slung seat in the cockpit, and reached with its right hand for a small, cute looking semi-automatic pistol encased in a polymer-type shoulder holster beneath its left axillary. It shouted what was probably an angry explicative.

Pulling back the slide of the pistol and letting it go forward, the slide slammed home a round into the pistol chamber, which the Goliath point-fired at Corporal Mercer immediately – missing.

The slide was driven to the rear of the pistol by the recoil, and when it was propelled forward by the recoil spring, a round was stripped from the magazine and failed to properly feed into the pistol chamber, resulting in a misfire.

The co-pilot seemed to be cursing, Mercer thought, as it worked frantically with both hands to clear the weapon and chamber another round. The cavalryman wasted no time in covering the short distance to the co-pilot and cleaving its skull unevenly down the middle with his unauthorized, non-regulation Bowie knife.

Corporal Mercer then assumed the copilot's seat. The soldier-turned-pilot found himself in front of a large cathode ray screen, which revealed that the spacecraft was in the earth's orbit.

Mercer grabbed the control stick that arose from the floor between his knees and tilted it to the left. The spacecraft violently leaned to the stern. Mercer tilted the stick back to the right but overcorrected.

188

The spacecraft dipped violently from left to right as he fought to stabilize the flight path into the enormous blue-green orb of the planet earth. The orb was completely filling the screen of the cathode ray screen.

Corporal Mercer's face was covered in beard stubble and shiny with sweat. His forehead was furrowed in concentration as he fought to control the shuddering spacecraft. His yellow bandana was knotted in the front, and covered the back of the neck, extending to between his shoulder blades. On either sleeve of his blue cavalry blouse blazed the gold of his corporal chevrons.

The blue cavalry uniform was made red, green then blue again as the strobe lights oscillated. The alarm strobe lights oscillated out of synchronization with the multiple alarms that sounded deafeningly throughout the ship. The warnings spoken in the female voice would become audible again as the blue whale warning cry receded to a distance, before returning in a crescendo of deafening intensity.

The automated alarm voice echoing in the backdrop added a surreal aspect to the unnatural hues cast onto the visage of the cavalryman's face. The intensity of his concentrated expression was accentuated by the alarm strobe lights.

The cavalryman was transformed into the epitome of patriotism as he tried to correct the violent list of the violently shaking flying saucer. He began flipping switches – he didn't have a clue what they were for.

He just flipped them. All of a sudden heavy metal rock music began playing.

It felt as though the space vessel would shake itself apart, but Mercer was an American! And Corporal Mercer was going to do it the right way – *the American way!*

Clouds were flying past the cathode ray screen with dizzying speed. Below, land masses sped by and Mercer could do nothing to slow the flying disc.

Multiple heavily armed fireteams of the rapid response team were arriving in the crew cabin now, and one of them settled into the seat beside Mercer and looked right at him. Mercer looked back, in return. They locked eyes for a split second…

Corporal Mercer pushed forward on the control stick, causing the craft to nose downward and the crewman to grab for his control stick. A violent struggle ensued for the control stick as the response team was flung violently about the cabin through centrifugal force. Heavy metal music mixed with the panoply of alarms that shrieked bedlam.

Far to the north, over the newly acquired territory of Alaska, a massive forest was flattened by the concussion of compressed sound as a brightly lit object of oscillating colors sped overhead, on an erratic course. Onward it hurled, speeding at low level over the Aleutian Islands before plunging into the Bering Sea. Silence reigned in the great American north once more.

Chapter Fourteen: Night Attack!

News of attack on the village of Chief Black Kettle by the 7th Cavalry had not been relayed to Fort Dodge, which lay far to the east.

There were dozens of angry, vengeful villages alongside the river, of which the inhabitants buzzed about like spiteful hornets shaken from their hives. Blood mixed with blocks of broken up ice in the Washita River, lending to it the aspect of a gigantic, grotesque Bloody Mary.

Dusk had settled early at Fort Dodge, Kansas. Fireplaces roared in the officers' quarters in which the Custer women continued to while the time away.

Libbie read a story aloud to Margaret and Beverly, by light of the sputtering whale oil lanterns. The lanterns were placed about the leather upholstered Chesterfield – a comfortable, spring loaded settee with fitted cushions.

The lamps were on pedestal type end tables made of lustrous black walnut specialized for that purpose. Eliza was cleaning the kitchen and its utensils as Libbie read from Nathaniel Hawthorne's "Young Goodman Brown."

"Oh! Wasn't that just appalling how the young wife poisoned her husband so that she could inherit all that was his!" chirped Libbie, pausing for a sip of piping hot tea from a prized porcelain teacup decorated with intricate designs.

"I think it was very shrewd of her," interpolated Beverly.

Margaret took her eyes momentarily from her sister in law and studied Beverly, being careful not to be seen doing so. As she appraised Beverly surreptitiously, she saw the suggestion of the deep, dividing valley that lay between her heavy, pendulous mounds. The brunette's loose cotton night shirt failed to completely ensconce the upper crevasse that separated the twin hillocks.

The moderate light from the smoking, sputtering lamps cast a strong shadow into the cleft between the dark-haired woman's defining features, accentuating their full form, highlighting the thimble sized prominences against the worn cotton fabric, Margaret thought.

From outside a fusillade of rifle fire erupted from one of the picket houses as the guards took a marauding band of winter clad Cheyenne under fire. The Indians returned fire and soon the exchange escalated into a full-blown firefight.

From the Spartan-like enlisted men's barracks soldiers ran cursing through knee deep snow, toward the picket houses – which were literally fortified stone towers twenty feet tall that had been constructed to provide interlocking fields of fire.

Automatic weapons fire exploded from the purple gloom, temporarily illuminating parts of the treeline as Comanche brought up a pair of captured Gatling guns to assist their Cheyenne allies.

The cast lead alloy bullets smacked into the granite blocks, sending sparks, then flying off as they ricocheted wildly into the night sky.

Some of the deadly bullets entered into the rifle embrasures, from which the soldiers fired madly, and bounced about with a spalling effect – ripping soldiers to pieces.

Even from within the warmth of security in the officers' quarters the muffled screams and explicatives could be heard as soldiers reeled before the Gatling guns.

Big soldiers, artillerymen more than six feet tall and weighing over two hundred pounds lugged field pieces into position and prepared to fire the cannon into the tree line when they were scythed down by the skillfully operated Gatling guns.

War-whooping masses of Cheyenne, Comanche and Sioux that lined the garbage strewn, uneven treeline that flanked the dirt road erupted like a tidal wave, in an almost unheard of night attack. The Gatling guns shifted their base of fire so as to not hit their own warriors.

Sinewy and tall, sixteen hundred Cheyenne led the attack across the frozen, white mantle of snow, followed by their smaller, but no less dangerous Comanche and Sioux cohorts.

Charismatic leaders wearing double trailer, ermine tubed war bonnets ran war-whooping through the snow followed by their hundreds as war drums began thrumming a crescendo of doom; the pounding of brown hands on leather war drums beat a death dirge on Fort Dodge.

Medicine men, livid with hallucinations from mushroom tea and made over-strong with adrenaline pulled the rusted iron grilles loose from the picket towers at the ground level, before entering the fortified structures, followed by their comrades.

The Cheyenne were much larger than their Native American cousins who had migrated down from Canada and Minnesota centuries before, owing to the incessant war of red man against red man.

The war painted faces of the braves bared their tobacco stained teeth and locked their obsidian eyes fiercely with the blue eyes of the soldiers as they came to grips with each other.

Not having time to reload, both sides fought with knives, and dug their dirty fingernails into each other's tracheas as they throttled one another in orgiastic hand to hand combat.

Piceous eyes squinted from behind the face smeared with black-hand marks on either cheek. The Dog Soldier crawled warily, on all fours, sniffing the floor of the block house. All around him his comrades fought the soldiers; the deadly fight remained undecided. He wore the blue cavalry trousers of a slain soldier, and the high-topped Wellington styled cavalry boots favored by officers. The warrior was a Cheyenne Dog Soldier - renowned for his keen sense of smell.

The long nose was hooked evilly at the tip, completing a sinister angle - like that of a turkey buzzard. The uncomplimentary nasal appendage extruded grotesquely from a hideous face that at once invoked the mental image of an animated cigar store Indian. The nostrils of the curvilinear nose flared urgently as it scented the air in response to a distinctive odor.

The Dog Soldier had been trained to scent out dynamite. And he was sure he had captured the tell-tale odor.

Eyes black as charcoal focused through eyelids narrowed into slits of animosity. The face stamped with the black-hand images lifted upward, slowly turning from side to side while the nose sniffed with nostrils flared. The Dog Soldier knew he was nearing the origin of the scent which assailed his keen olfactory organ.

Crawling on all fours he sniffed the ground like a hound, his nose pushing aside spent ammunition copper casings that almost completely covered the floor of the abandoned room he now entered. Certain that his keen sense of smell had led him to the cache of dynamite he'd been tasked with finding, the warrior stopped. The Dog Soldier's face was contorted into a mask of repugnance as it hovered directly over the reeking piss bucket of malfeasant urine.

"The pistols! Get the pistols quickly!" shouted Libbie, setting aside her macabre bed time story, she added, "They are upon us! The Indians are within the fortress compound!"

"It's a compound show down!" exclaimed Margaret, running upstairs for her revolver.

The Indians, a confederation of loosely allied tribes usually led by Cheyenne would appear for a raid of one week or two in a specific area during the winter and move on. Usually they marauded in small war parties of twenty to several hundred braves. To attack a fortress town with a force numbering in the thousands, in the darkness and in snow was atypical.

The intrigues that transpired among the elder chiefs and sachems on the Tribal Councils revolved around seizing warbrides these days. To be able to raid a fort and take all of its women would ensure a large number of pregnancies the following spring – and just in time for the demonic fertility rites.

These were rites performed by gifted medicine men in tepees sheathed in the tanned hides of their enemies and sung to demoniacal effigies with their characteristic exaggerated anatomy.

The intertribal politics that pervaded the marijuana smoke filled tepees of the Cheyenne High Council were more and more centered on high risk gambles for captive white women and children.

The children could be brought up as Cheyenne and the women could bear many offspring. The estimates that probably one half of their braves were white men who had been raised as Cheyenne did not bother them. Nor did the fact that most of the wives of the young braves were abducted white women.

Elizabeth and Margaret Custer made sure that the percussion caps were seated tightly on their Remington and Colt Army revolvers. Beverly had a Smith and Wesson Model 1, which was a .22 caliber revolver. Its advantage lay in the fact that it could be reloaded using copper shells as opposed to the time consumptive ramming of powder and ball.

The patent owned by Smith and Wesson on bored through revolver cylinders made it necessary for Colt and Remington to continue with the obsolescent cap and ball design.

Soldiers, flushed out from their stone block houses beat on the door of the Custer quarters. Some of them continued to shoot at the approaching natives while several others joined those pounding urgently on the heavy, oak double doors.

"Let us in! Open up and let us in! The Indians have taken the outer works!" shouted one of the soldiers. Several soldiers were firing Spencer repeating rifles in an unequal response against the Henry repeating rifles of the Native Americans.

The tubular magazine of the Henry held fifteen rounds, and with a bullet in the chamber it carried sixteen. Also, the working of the lever action served to cock back the hammer in addition to eject and load a new round, unlike with the Spencer.

"No!" Libbie warned Beverly. "You mustn't let them in! "The Cheyenne will pour in here. You know what they want – women with which to breed – *warbrides!*"

The plaintive pleas of the soldiers were carried away in an arctic blast of wind as they fled for their lives from the expansive, veranda style porch of the Custer quarters. They were rapidly being shot down by Cheyenne who fired from the shoulder, in the standing-offhand position. Other soldiers were fleeing in the blood-stained snow, waist deep in places.

Moments later, the jingle of boot mounted spurs announced a retinue of Indians confidently mounting the wooden veranda of the officers' quarters.

The Native Americans reflected a hybrid image of the Stone Age blended into the Industrial Age. Many were dressed in aboriginal, cave man like winter attire yet carried state of the art modern weapons.

The veranda had been meticulously shoveled clear of snow and ice by Eliza, and the horrifying footsteps of some of the braves could be heard upon the thick oak planking.

The headman was a tall, well-formed warrior chief; his leather breeches and wolf skins could not hide the muscular contours of his athletic physique, sculpted by years of woodcraft and horsemanship.

The scarred face, made evil looking through the application of war paint in a series of bold stripes, betrayed no emotion.

The chief's war bonnet extended proportionately from either temple of the broad head. The mature bald eagle feathers were knitted into the pelt of a rabbit skin skullcap – lavishly girded by the thickset firecrackers of white and scarlet canister like coverings. These were wrapped tightly near the bottom of every feather. The tops of the eagle feathers had yellow dyed pony hair affixed and at the area where the tufts connected to the feather tips. Sewn onto the front of the rabbit skin skullcap was a magnificent brow band - a frontal strip two inches wide consisting of multicolored beads. The beads had been sewn in intricate patterns of tepees and swastikas. At least a dozen copper hawk bells attached to the brow band jingled with the sudden movements of the warrior's head as he mounted the veranda.

There was fear within the quarters where the white women listened with growing alarm to the Cheyenne and Sioux men talking amongst each other.

Behind the headman followed a chanting, malevolent medicine man who mumbled hallucinogen induced incantations. The medicine man's face was heavily tattooed with geometric design and to either side of him were stalwart warriors dressed in buffalo skin coats, buckskin trousers and either cavalry boots or leather moccasins reinforced with rawhide soles.

The long, browned, tobacco stained teeth of the Cheyenne war chief had been filed to points and the flesh of some unfortunate soldier clung tenaciously between them. The sneering mouth of the chief was made more sinister as he ran his tongue over the fangs, evoking the specter of a wolf who sought to lick its chops.

Two dozen more young toughs, armed with Henry and Spencer repeating rifles followed the chief and the medicine man up the steps. The braves fanned out in a haughty, swaggering manner to either side of the two leaders on the sweeping veranda.

Within the fortress compound itself several thousand other warriors found their advance held up by the fields of unrelenting, desperately interlocking fire from the resisting blockhouses.

There were no rules of war to hinder the Native American combatants who had mounted the 2x12 inch oak planks that made up the stair case leading to the portico porch.

The braves who wore thick, flexible rawhide double soled moccasins found the footwear very much suited to the icy weather and these left their imprints on the ice crusted snow that covered the slippery steps. These heavily insulated moccasins were decorated in beads and kept the feet warm and dry, owing to the application of bear fat.

Most of the braves were young, half white warriors – an almost equal number were full Caucasian, taken as children and formally adopted into Cheyenne families.

Now that the aboriginal ensemble had succeeded in attaining temporary safety, their means of breaching the massive oak double doors to the Custers' quarters was the primary object. A Sioux brave, perhaps a head shorter than his compatriots, but stoutly built, raised his Henry to shoot into the handle of the door.

"No!" commanded the headman, placing his hand on the hot barrel of the rifle and gently pressing it downward. "You might hit the women."

The effort of the main attack was beginning to fail. The impetus of the screaming horde was blunted in an orgasm of flying cerebral matter, twitching limbs and spilled viscera.

Another banzai-like attack accompanied with whooping and frenzied foot motions carried the shrinking assault element into a merciless *metal storm* of interlocking fields of fire. It was the interlocking fields of fire that was chewing up the main aggregation of the attacking force.

This caused the main body of Indians to splinter into large groups and try to skirt around the soldier filled block houses.

The braves who stood on the wide-open veranda of the Custer front porch realized that they were running out of time. Impatiently they regarded the stolidity of the overbuilt wooden double doors.

Spurs jingled menacingly on the heels of many of the warriors who wore captured cavalry boots. They spoke urgently as they paced the length of the veranda, seeking some means of entrance.

The two leaders – the chief and the medicine man had arrived at the decision to force the double doors. The chief was of a flat affect and seemed emotionless. The Sioux medicine man was foaming at the mouth, speaking in tongues to his entities.

What the chief and medicine man were expecting to find within the officers' quarters were terrified, submissive *warbrides.*

"Do you think the Indians will pass us by in their rush to take the fort?" Margaret asked Libbie Custer who studied the heavy oak double doors with trepidation and dilated pupils. She appreciated the heavy, overbuilt doors made of red oak and enjoyed the reassurance that the full sized, balanced revolver in the palm of her sweating right hand gave her.

"No, dear Margaret; they most certainly will not. The objects of their passions are to be found here – standing anxiously within this parlor. We are poor little wounded things that need a place to hide, but instead must stand our ground. We must abide in this eyrie, like eagles rather than fledgling sparrows.

"Wait until I say otherwise, and then we will let loose upon them like Valkyries! At the final moment, when hope seems forlorn, we will egress upstairs to my bedchamber," answered the wife of Lieutenant Colonel Custer.

"Oh, and how brave you are, Libbie!" exclaimed Margaret.

"I suspect this is not the first time you have had to shoot a man!" Margie said admiringly.

"My father, Judge Bacon, allowed me to shoot a condemned prisoner once," replied Libbie.

"The villain feared the noose and begged to be shot," Libbie explained, adding, "and so my father asked me if I would like the honor."

"They're just males, Libbie – animals," answered Margaret. "Red men, white men, black men – it makes not any difference. All men are filthy and ignorant of the Law of Moses; unclean heathens."

Margaret bitterly remembered in the instant, when she had come upon Charles Scholten taking the photos – photos of her sister-in-law with the enormous black man named Don L, who did errands and chores for the wives of the officers when they were in the field.

It was suspected, but only whispered among the wives, that some of their number employed the gigantic Negro for chores of a more intimate nature.

"What's going on in here!?" Margaret had shouted, startling the trio and placing the black man in fear for his life.

Margaret's attention was drawn from the unwholesome memory and back to the present as her eyes focused on the knob of the left double door.

Tentatively at first, the pewter door knob shook as an unseen hand tried it. Then it began to rattle and shake fiercely as a scarred, tattooed hand on the other side tried to force it. Then the other door knob was tried in vain. A moment later both were simultaneously shaken so violently as to threaten to break the knobs loose from the doors.

"I'm gonna put my eyeball up to the keyhole an see what we are facin' Miss Libbie!" exclaimed Eliza, walking bravely up to the door and kneeling down to peer through a key hole. What Eliza beheld beggared her imagination as she sprung upward, reeling backwards. She would have fallen if not for the steadying hands of Beverly.

"Oh, my Lord!" screamed Eliza, placing her hands to her chest, "I think I am havin' the big one! I think I am havin' a heart O-tack! Miss Libbie! Dey was an eyeball lookin' right back at me tru dat keyhole!"

"Eliza! *HURRY!* - go up to my bedchamber! Load all of the general's hunting rifles and find all the cartridges you can! Lay them all on the bed where we can get to them!

There was nothing visible of the pampered, helpless child-woman now as Elizabeth Custer maintained control of the escalating situation.

"Yes, Ma'am, Miss Libbie! I swear I believe I was lookin' into the eyeball of the ol' Devil his self!" responded the wide-eyed Eliza, still clutching at her chest.

Margaret's Colt Army Model 1860 was held in both hands with the hammer cocked back and she was pointing it straight at the heavy double door which was shaking and reeling from powerful kicks.

Libbie held her Remington .44 caliber New Army revolver in her right hand. The hammer was thumbed back into the cocked position.

Eliza peered into the unlit closet, looking for the shotgun. The twin barreled fowling piece stood leaning into a corner, and she found it only by reaching through the numerous uniforms of the Boy General.

"I gots it!" Eliza shouted jubilantly, hasting toward the door of the bedroom while cradling the English double barrel percussion shotgun. The Samuel Southerland double barrel was fully loaded and set to fire with percussion caps. The blued, twin thirty-one-inch Damascus steel barrels shone lustrously in the light of the lanterns.

The walls of the parlor room were covered in a loud, bright wall paper with indeterminate floral designs. The paper had begun to come loose in places, and it shook with the urgent, incessant pounding that had begun to unhinge the door and splinter the wood.

Libbie's long, auburn colored hair was untied and spilled loosely down over her lithe, strongly built shoulders. This added an Aegean, Hellenistic aspect to the classical beauty of the woman. The diminutive light cast from the whale oil lanterns cast shadows that emphasized the contours of her exquisitely defined face.

Elizabeth Bacon Custer's face was sculpted beneath a high, intelligent forehead. Eyebrows which were plucked into thin wisps furrowed in concentration. The full, pretty lips were tightly pressed together as she focused her gray blue eyes on the failing double doors. The nostrils of the petite nares flared with adrenaline. The exquisite nose was joined on either side by full, rounded cheeks. The chin was small, the jawline well set and strong.

The doors shook fiercely from the forceful pounding and began to splinter loose from their hinges. They were fracturing now and suddenly the double doors flew wide open. Although it lasted for only a fraction of a second, in the minds of the women present in that room the moment was anchored in perpetuity.

The big chief and the medicine man stood framed against the open doorway with the reassurance of dozens of braves behind and to either side of them. They stood for a moment awed by the lethal beauty that stood redoubtably before them.

It was a moment they should not have wasted. It was Margaret who shot first, hitting the stalwart chief in the center of the chest. The enormous Cheyenne dropped his rifle and clutched his chest with both hands and groaned loudly, orgasm-like. His thin lips, dyed purple with berry juice, drew back and revealed his sharpened teeth in all their horror.

Margaret thumbed back the hammer of the single action .44 caliber revolver and shot him again, and again, the distinguishing features of her upper torso jiggled perceptibly beneath her nearly open robe each time the gun recoiled.

With his eyes fixed on her pendulous mammillae, the Cheyenne war chief stepped forward robotically each time one of the nearly one-ounce slugs tore into him. Margaret's fleshy hams flexed together and relaxed each time she squeezed the trigger.

"I hears a shootin' down there!" shouted Eliza from the master bedroom upstairs, "An I am comin' with the general's double barrel shot gun! An it's a loaded with the double ought buckshot!"

Libbie Custer aimed, carefully aligning the blade of the revolver's front site onto the medicine man's sloping forehead and ignored the big chief, who fell forward in a heap.

The chief looked with clouding eyes, seeing for the last time, that Margaret Custer's robe had completely opened. The bamboozled Cheyenne war chief stared at the almost palm sized brown halos that helped to define Margaret's swaying features as she fumbled with her gun. The pigmented glands were punctuated in their center with thimble sized prominences.

Seeing Libbie Custer aiming the revolver directly at his head, the medicine man adeptly stepped back and to the side, in an evasive movement akin to that of the praying- mantis.

This medicine man had thick black hair. The hairline began below the low set forehead, and was tightly braided into a single ponytail, secured with a strip of red cloth. His archaic face bore a scarred, Philistine-like visage. A thin, dirty scar from a long-ago tomahawk attack extended at an angle down from his right earlobe. The scar traversed beneath his cheek and terminated at the outer side of his chin. The scar indented where it crossed the bony structures of the face, implying the tomahawk had cloven into bone.

Air hissed between the medicine man's teeth like a snake as he stepped behind the wall. The quick reflexed, fast thinking holy man remained on the porch, behind the wall and prepared to make his next nefarious move.

Elizabeth pulled the hair trigger and sent the .44 caliber lead bullet flying into the face of the brave who had been standing immediately behind the medicine man. The brave's hands flew to the dime sized hole to the right of his nose and his scream was a gurgle as he turned and tried to staunch the wound. The other braves pushed past him and rushed into a *metal storm* of gun fire.

Half a dozen stalwart braves dressed in all manner of winter clothing fell writhing to the floor as Elizabeth and Beverly emptied their revolvers. It seemed that no matter which brave they shot, another appeared to take his place. The warriors made no attempt to kill the women; *they wanted them alive.*

"Dis un's fo' you! An' you!" shouted Eliza, causing the painted faces of two warriors to look up at her.

The brave on the right looked up the stairwell at the black woman who aimed a shotgun at him. His head was covered in a wolf skin scalp, including the ears, and was still attached to the main skin, the fur of which comprised a coat. A large scar from a knife fight began at his hairline and extended vertically down his sloped forehead, then altered course and arced across his right eye and terminated where the jaw meets with the neck. Although he was completely blind in the ruined eye, he could see well enough with the other.

He, along with his cohort peered through the reeking fog of gun smoke before the buckshot compromised the integrity of their skulls.

The headless warriors stamped madly about, feeling with tattooed hands all about their shoulders. Frantically they felt for their heads, which had been displaced and transplanted directly to the cheerfully decorative wall paper behind them.

"Looks like dey doin' a lil' scalp dance, Miss Libbie!" shouted Eliza.

"Libbie! Do we run upstairs for the bedroom?!" shouted Beverly.

"Yes!" answered Elizabeth Custer.

Margaret bought time for the other women by emptying every chamber of her .22 S&W Model 1 into a thick winter coat that covered a sweating, hairless chest. Quickly, she extracted the spent copper casings of the diminutive little revolver.

The heavy buffalo coats slowed the velocity of the tiny .22 caliber short bullets, rendering them ineffective. Beverly did not have time to reload the Model 1 and turned to take flight up the staircase. That was when the medicine man reappeared and grabbed her by the night shirt, ripping it from her and revealing her in totality.

That her complete natural state was revealed was not all. The medicine man stood frozen in fear at the red, crescent shaped hemangioma on her plump, fleshy posterior, sheening with perspiration.

All of the braves, for there were dozens in the parlor now, stood staring in abject horror at the birthmark.

Some shielded their faces, while others made an "O" with their thumb and forefinger, then spat through it; the sign of the Evil Eye.

"Get out of here!" shouted Beverly. *"You know who I am!"*

The braves fled out of the parlor and into the cold wastes as though they were carried by the wind.

Chapter Fifteen: Debaucheress!

The eyes of Beverly were black, liquid pools which conveyed a surreal, almost palpable malignance.

Quickly, she wrapped the nightshirt sarong style about her muscular haunch to hide the odious nevus.

"The mark of the Devil," whispered Margaret Custer, the utterance provoked Beverly to look up and lock eyes with her. Margie averted the wild, penetrating stare which was enhanced by the black, disheveled hair.

The Devil's Mark, as it was called in ages old wives tales, was placed at birth upon a bride to a demon. These brides were said through generations of folklore to be born witches and that the mark was insensitive to pain.

In antiquity it was the usual practice to put such a one with the crescent mark to death. These birthmarks were hidden on the body and a person suspected of having one could be stripped of clothing, and if need be, shaven in order to find the mark.

Beverly's father and mother had kept the birthmark secret, and terrified of their child's deep perception of people's thoughts, believed the mark to be what it appeared to be.

While not suspected of anything bad or unseemly, Beverly did seem to be able to read other people's thoughts, see through walls, and cause objects to move through force of will. But following the advice of her worried parents, she kept these phenomena to herself and nothing ever came of it.

Gnarled, lifeless trees stood gauntly, like grim sentinels, casting their nighted shadows across the blood-stained snow under the wan, intermittent moonlight. Eliza watched over the sleeping Custer women like a she-wolf.

As the hours trudged inexorably by, the dull nickel light of a subdued morning sun fought its way through the snow laden clouds. This in no way diminished the reality of what lurked in the unfathomable depths of that primordial tree line that stood away from the fort.

"Unnnngh!" mumbled Beverly when something had awakened her. Beverly had tried to sit up reflexively in the bed, but found Margaret lying partially across her. Both women were in pull over night shirts.

Feeling something on her person, Beverly seized Margaret's thumb and forefinger, bending them fiercely back and causing Margie to recoil and cry out.

"Stop it – you're hurting me! You're going to break my fingers!" cried out Margaret.

"You touched me! *How dare you!*" riposted Beverly.

"I was talking to you, I thought you were awake and Oh! Let go of my fingers or I'll claw you!" shouted Margie.

I'll break them! Talking to me and you thought I was awake! Pervert!" exclaimed Beverly and bending the fingers further back the thumb slipped loose, but the index finger popped loudly as it dislocated.

Jumping out of the bed, Margaret tried to reposition the throbbing finger back into place, sobbing.

"Oh, look what you've done! *You've broken it!* All that I was trying to do Beverly," explained Margaret, "was relate to you a story passed onto me by a close friend. She spoke of the livelihood of those fabled Japanese women – the mermaid-like amas. They are those women who swim wearing naught but a tether and who dive into the depths to procure the oyster. Then the oyster yields to the diver the lustrous pearl within its fleshy folds!"

"The next time an ama rubs the pearl of a sleeping mermaid she will most assuredly lose the fingers that ease into the oyster's fold!" warned Beverly.

"You broke my finger for no good reason!" shouted Margaret viciously. *"You broke it!"*

Margaret's thigh was bent at the knee as she propped one foot on the bed, and the other on the floor, leaning forward into her raised knee and grasping her injured finger.

With no warning, Beverly grabbed Margaret by the hair and using both hands pulled the woman's head forward. Margaret cursed when Beverly's hands pulled large clump of hair loose from the roots. Her head snapped back violently with the release of tension, causing her face to contort grotesquely into a paroxysm of rage.

Instead of fleeing the room, Margaret lurched forward onto Beverly, grabbing for her throat. Beverly grasped Margie's wrists, easily breaking the grip, but was constrained beneath the larger woman.

The two women cursed and shrieked as they fought. It was with the limber flexibility of a contortionist with which Beverly turned the table on Margaret. Beverly had executed a 180-degree repositioning beneath her raging antagonist. The dark-haired woman writhed like a snake, inching her head beneath the mossy grotto that rubbed brusquely across her grimaced visage. It was when her shoulders had cleared the sweating, flexing haunches that Beverly reached into her adversary's most intimate sanctum.

Margaret leapt up, both hands clutching between her legs, staunching the crimson flow.

"Debaucheress!" screamed Margie, aghast at what had Beverly had done. "You wear the very crown of my sanctity upon your hand!"

Someone opened the door and entered the room without the courtesy of knocking.

"Margaret! What has come over you!? If you were not my husband's sister I would turn you out onto the snow!" exclaimed Libbie, who had entered the room upon hearing the tumult.

The fighting ceased upon the appearance of Elizabeth. Libbie had a "command presence" when around women that was always palpable. Though it was not recognized by men, it was by women.

"The woman has a hold of me, sister," answered Margaret, wiping the blood from herself with the front of her night shirt, "I am beside myself and my blood burns. She sets me on fire."

"Then mayhap we will see this ardor extinguished like a flame – put out with the caresses of my husband's belt!" threatened Elizabeth Custer. Beverly had never seen Libbie speak to Margie in such a way.

Although Margaret's attempt at Beverly had been defeated most cruelly, her attention was now drawn to Libbie.

Libbie had procured one of her husband's thin leather belts, one that was meant to wear beneath a gun belt and hold up the trousers. She clenched the tanned cincture in her left hand. She was pointing her right hand and angrily stabbing the index finger at her sister in law as she admonished her.

"You're just like a man!" shouted Libbie, "Filthy, no good man!" The thin, tanned leather of the slender belt waved menacingly toward Margaret.

"Wat dem mean girls done dun to you, Miss Margaret?" soothed Eliza as she entered through the doorway, holding a heavy house robe.

Margaret walked toward Eliza, who led her out of the room.

"I apologize for the actions of my husband's sister; it is in part my fault that she behaves in such an aberrant manner," admitted Libbie.

Libbie approached the strange, dark woman, whose night shirt was torn. Somehow during the struggle, the shirt had been ripped, exposing the back, but not the front. Beverly was incognizant of this.

"Please, it's nothing," said Beverly, alarmed and with no room to back up, "pay me no mind."

"Turn around, let me see, you're all scratched up – oh! That mark! It – it – it's *THE MARK OF THE DEVIL!!!*" exclaimed Libbie.

"Yes, it is," answered Beverly.

Beverly's eyes were black as coal, thought Libbie. Libbie looked into the sloe eyes, and at the white, crooked teeth. It was common that with so many people their teeth became crowded and snaggled with the growth of wisdom teeth.

"She's a pretty woman," Libbie thought, "in a certain way that's hard to define."

"Yes, I am," responded Beverly.

"You read my mind! Oh Lord – a Demoness! A witch!" exclaimed Elizabeth Custer. She felt faint, weak. She needed to sit down before she passed out. The room was moving, she could not stand up.

"Sit down on my bed," said Beverly, in a soft voice that was a not a request.

"Do you want to look at my birthmark?" asked Beverly.

Then Beverly added sagely, as only one with the "sight" can, "I *know* that you *do.*"

Beverly stepped very close to the seated Libbie Custer, and revealing her crescent mark to Libbie's face, Beverly asked:

"What do you think of my little birthmark?"

"I – I think it is unique, it is a gift. It is said that the moon as viewed in Hell always appears thus, as in this birthmark. It is beautiful!" answered Libbie.

"Then adore it!" commanded Beverly…

Chapter Sixteen: Bareknuckle Debacle!

The president, known for his volatile temper and fits of uncontrollable rage, was trembling with fury.

"Fort Dodge was attacked and nearly overwhelmed in spite of Custer's raid into Oklahoma!" exclaimed President Johnson.

Johnson had a bizarre, complex friendship with the Custers. George Armstrong Custer was one of the few national figures held in high respect who openly endorsed and defended the hated president. And Andrew Johnson had more than admiration for Custer's wife, Libbie Bacon Custer.

The entire nation venerated Libbie Custer as much as they did George Armstrong, prompting the maligned, misunderstood president to cultivate their friendship.

President Johnson could count his real friends on the fingers of one hand. The despot knew he could count on Custer, because he remembered - he remembered the day not so long ago, back in September 1866.

Johnson had gone by presidential train through part of the country on a month long public attempt to recruit support for his post war reconstruction policies directed toward the South.

General Grant and Lieutenant Colonel Custer, along with his wife Libbie were accompanying President Johnson on the steam locomotive. Grant remained reclusive and never would stand at the numerous stops and stump for the president. However, Custer would.

The disastrous speaking tour devolved into a grotesque, self-aggrandizing oratory campaign. The vitriolic diatribe communicated by the inebriated President Johnson degenerated into shouting matches with hecklers. And in a reoccurring theme the president was frequently comparing himself to Jesus even as he flung obscenities at his detractors.

The querulous, disparaging speaking engagements grew increasingly opprobrious – and precarious. Hundreds of protesters were tragically killed when the platform they stormed in an attack on the president collapsed. They plunged to their unhappy demise, drowning in a fetid, swampy morass.

The presidential train slowly eased away as it gathered steam and escaped. All the while with Johnson peeking through the curtains of his window and clutching his revered Remington revolver.

But it was in Ohio that Johnson saw the extent of loyalty displayed by Lieutenant Colonel Custer really for the first time. While General Grant in effect was keeping his distance from the hated POTUS, Custer would step out on the campaign train and defend him.

"Get away from my president!" shouted the Yellow Hair at the dozens of riff-raff and white trash who stood cursing and jeering President Johnson.

"Cock sucker!" one of the constituents of the bawdy group yelled at President Johnson.

"I'll have your ass for that insult!" exclaimed Johnson, angrily stepping down from the podium.

"Make way for me!" threatened the drunken Commander in Chief at the Secret Service men, shoving his way through them.

"Which one of you worthless pigs called me a cock sucker?! Which one of you is the traitor that just signed his own fuckin' death warrant? Which one of you is it?!" demanded the president, as he approached the dangerous, unpredictable group of thugs. He approached with the gait of a man who is sure of himself, and confident in all of his ways.

Brusque guffawing exploded from the burgeoning throng that had immediately enlarged by hundreds. Thousands more were spilling onto the streets, eager to disrupt the president's speaking event.

President Andrew Johnson scrutinized the derisory, sarcastic ensemble with rummy, pig-like eyes. They shifted from right to left, taking the measure of each man's strength individually.

"Maybe it was you!" The president exclaimed, seizing the largest man of the rabble rousers by the shirt collar and gun belt. Easily hoisting the six-foot five-inch, three-hundred-pound hoodlum over his head like a sack of horse feed. The president turned and strode several steps toward the railway track, hurling the twisting, cursing man onto one of the shining, silvery rails.

"My back!" screamed the prostrate troublemaker at the bleak, pale sun adding, "The tyrant has broken my back! My arms and legs are insensitive! I am immobile!"

"See what that got him?" laughed Johnson, smiling as he approached the hecklers once more, adding, "he signed his own fucking death warrant! Hear him down there hollering? What's he going to do about that?"

"Be careful of them!" Custer warned President Johnson.

"They're the ones who better be careful!" Johnson answered Custer.

Suddenly the air was electrified by the rifle shot crack of a bull whip as the Boy General plied the leather to the malcontents. They eased away, arms raised protectively, shielding their faces from the flecking tip of the bull whip which uncannily struck repeatedly like a rattlesnake.

The president grabbed a short, heavy set man dressed in bibbed dungaree overalls who was stuffing a dirty handkerchief into a bleeding, empty eye socket.

"I'm going to beat you like a red-headed stepson!" laughed the insane President Johnson, showing strong, tobacco stained teeth.

Press reporters noted that the POTUS was raging like a lunatic.

"Eat this!" the president shouted, slamming his fist into the man's pudgy, unshaven face. The blow was like that of a pile driver, as the impact drove loose, bad teeth beyond the tonsils and deep into the gullet of the man's throat.

"I was born two miles and a half from here, but I am ashamed of you!" shouted the Boy General at the seething mob. He wielded the whip as though he were an experienced mule skinner. Noses, ears, and flesh flew from faces contorted in fear and hate.

Snapping back to the present, President Johnson looked with appreciation upon the daguerreotypes of the pretty lady smiling into the eye of the camera. Johnson began perusing through the entire stack, going over each one individually, and slowly – very, very slowly...

"Pinkerton! If Fort Dodge is in danger from the Cheyenne – then I want to be there! Right in the thick of it!" exclaimed Johnson, sliding the drawer of the desk closed.

"Yes Sir, Mr. President," answered Pinkerton, who knew better than to question the spontaneous, rash and irresponsible statement.

"Let's head out to the frontier!" reiterated Johnson, suddenly jovial.

The president's demeanor frequently fluctuated from uncontrolled rage to tranquility. Sometimes these polar opposite emotions would be replaced with a brooding silence in which schizophrenia rendered the man unreachable.

An hour later found the *JUGGERNAUT* headed west under full steam. President Johnson was ascending and descending a series of mood swings on the presidential train, as he spoke with General Grant in a one-way conversation that saw Grant only getting in rebuttals piecemeal.

"To know me is to hate me! Did you hear about the way I lit into that guy that pulled a knife on me?" the president had laughingly asked the recuperating General Grant.

Johnson was alluding to an infamous incident in which he had blinded a man in a brawl that occurred in Baltimore, Maryland. The event had occurred when the train had stopped to take on water and replenish its coal bunkers at a depot in Baltimore.

Naturally enough – for the president anyway, he had seized upon the opportunity to go into town "incognito."

"That much is true," Grant said, adding, "to know you *is* to hate you."

President Johnson elaborated to General Grant that he had been walking the town after hours dressed as a bum, to avoid recognition. Nevertheless, he was shadowed closely by his Irish and Scots bodyguards. Those men flitted surreptitiously like grim, evil specters through the shadows. Shadows that cast from the wavering light of gas street lights. But then - suddenly he was recognized!

"I'm proud of my ascendancy from poverty to the White House," Johnson affably said to Grant, his personality changing again, his topic of conversation was chameleon; ever changing.

"Of course you are," agreed Grant, not fully sure which direction that the unpredictable POTUS would take the conversation. "It was as though", thought General Grant, "the president had multiple personalities."

"The Working Man's Man," quipped Johnson, adding as an afterthought, "I am – the American Dream!"

"That's a crock of shit!" retorted Grant, the belligerence in the tone of the general's voice caused the president to guffaw in a robust burst of laughter.

"I like to sometimes dress in informal, but tailored clothing and venture out to speak with 'my' fellow countrymen," said Johnson to his unwilling listener.

"I know that you do," replied Grant, adding, "you like to go around picking fights."

Ulysses S. Grant's broken right arm was cast in plaster of Paris, and in a sling. It throbbed constantly, and the general was continually drunk in an effort to assuage the pulsating pain.

"Three of them set themselves upon me – like pit bulls! And before my security team could reach me, I had hit that loudmouth so smartly in his face that I severed his optic nerves and blinded him! I whipped his two accomplices roundly before I was pulled off of them!

"But then," interrupted General Grant, "Radical Republicans seized on the opportunity to slander you in national newspapers, accusing you of dressing like a bum to avoid recognition and beg drinks like a ne'er do well."

"So what!" laughed the president, continuing his self-absorbed conversation, "I'm hoping that the next town the train has to stop in to take on coal and water has a fisticuffs! I need to let off a little steam and get some exercise! Pinkerton said there's a contest for a belt at one of the next stops."

The nine-car train had a massive portrait of President Johnson above the enormous cast iron cattle guard attached to the front of the Baldwin Locomotive

226

Works 4-4-0 steam engine. Thrusting out boldly from either side of the plow-like cattle guard was a pair of large American flags, snapping briskly at forty-five-degree angles to the right and left of the scowling portraiture of the president.

The presidential train that sped forward, sometimes plowing through herds of buffalo was the epitome of 19th Century technology.

The wide spacing of the axels allowed a voluminous boiler to be emplaced above the wheels, and the rotund boiler thrust outboard over them. The enhanced heating capacity of the boiler allowed much more power and traction than in the earlier English models that dominated the infancy of the American rail system.

The 4-4-0 was named thusly to denote its eight-wheel arrangement of four large wheels behind four smaller ones, with no wheels trailing. This was such a successful design that it caught on world-wide and would eventually become known as the "American type."

Black smoke bellowed from the rotund spark arrestor stack. An enormous headlight was mounted on a platform in front of the belching smoke stack. There was a large reflector to enlarge the weak oil flame that provided the beam.

The rail gauge was four feet, eight and one-half inches. Lore had it that the spacing between the wheels of Roman chariots is what the rail gauge was based on. This measurement was widely used in

England and carried over to America, which earlier in the century would buy all of its steam locomotives from England.

It was the next day, as the steam powered train replenished its coal bunkers and topped off the water boiler that the POTUS was dressed as a spectator in the rough-shod crowd that thronged around the elevated wooden platform. Atop the wooden platform that served as the ring were two combatants in a brutal bare knuckle pugilistic contest against one another. Johnson's security detail was placed strategically amongst the mob of rowdy onlookers.

The winner, a pugilist named Bill Skinner was a dangerous looking, oversized brute. Skinner's muscles rippled beneath his skin like those of a tiger as he flexed his eighteen-inch biceps to the roar of the crowd. The victorious athlete weighed 260 pounds and stood at six feet, three inches. He offered to take on any of the cheering crowd who had the money and was brave enough to face him in the ring.

"Any one of you wants to take me on," exclaimed Skinner, "$500 is what it'll cost you! Come on now, if you haven't got the money, borrow it! Steal it! Prostitute your wife! But that's what it'll cost you!"

The champion was truly a dangerous man. His black hair was shorn close to the bullet shaped head to deny purchase to his opponent. His ears were cauliflowered from having been struck with great force many times through countless combats. And his nose was flattened from long ago having been broken and not reset. The close set, darting eyes scanned the crowd for any takers, and then saw a bearded ruffian pushing his way forward, through the throng of hoodlums, miscreants and ne'er do wells that comprised the majority of the spectators.

There were not many women present, on account of the bone chilling cold weather, but what few there were would not pass for Sunday school teachers. They drank bottled beer and laughed raucously as they frolicked among their opposite sex.

President Johnson was an avid bare-knuckle fist fighting enthusiast. The five-foot ten-inch, two-hundred-pound president had taken up the challenge, entering the ring dressed as a ranch-hand and wearing a glued on, fake beard. He shoved the money into the hand of Bill Skinner's fight manager.

A thundering applause arose from the crowd, many of them were discharging their revolvers into the air. Half empty bottles of whiskey passed hand to hand. Cheap beer, made cold by the outdoor weather, flowed in abundance in this outpost of civilization in the Weird, Weird West.

The referee looked as though he could have been a competitor as well; standing six feet tall and built like a brick shit house. His grim, dark unshaven features were partially hidden by the broad rim of a dogged, worn out Union slouch hat. The hat was frayed in many places along the five-inch rim and seemed to compliment the handsome face.

"ARE YOU READY TO RUMMMMMMMMMMMMBLE???" the referee shouted through cupped hands, to amplify his voice. He shouted to the crowd, to incite excitement preluding the contest.

"This fight will be governed by the London Prize Ring Rules, established in 1838!" shouted the referee, who continued, "Under the set of twenty-nine rules, each round has no time limit! A round is ended when a contestant is knocked or wrestled to the ground! Biting, gouging and kicking are forbidden!"

The two contestants were seated and regarded each other fiercely within the twenty-four feet rectangle shaped ring. Two ropes were affixed to wooden posts. A chalk scratch line was drawn across the floor of the ring, and upon the referee's command, the fighters would advance to it and shake hands.

While the referee spoke, the contenders were seated in their corners on diminutive, three legged stools. Spectators leaned into the ropes in order to poke and feel their muscles, like horse traders plying the flesh of prize stock.

The champion was seated in the corner with his back to the sun, forcing the President of the United States to squint, adding an even more malevolent aspect to his already villainous countenance.

Stripped down to his black, long handle style fighting britches, red stockings and lace up fighting boots, the champion's body reflected the results of nearly a decade of fighting in the ring. He had the physique of a Farnese Hercules, with not an ounce of superfluous

230

flesh on him. Burr headed and smooth shaven but for a handle bar mustache, he was the penultimate in 19th Century pugilistic development.

The Commander in Chief on the other hand, being dressed as he was, was more difficult to assess. Johnson was wearing a fake beard to disguise his identity. He wore a tan muslin long sleeved shirt with the sleeves rolled up, for britches he wore a set of rare blue denim trousers developed by a Bavarian immigrant named Levi Strauss. Johnson's denim jeans had a cowboy cut to accommodate his steerhide pointed toe cowboy boots.

The spectators could see that Johnson was clearly a brawler, but no one suspected he could be a serious contender. If the president had not had such a firm gut, he could have passed for an "evil Santa Claus."

"Fighters advance to the scratch line!" shouted the referee.

The mob consisted of hundreds of blood-thirsty spectators. The rowdy crowd was madly placing bets on how long into the first round the ubiquitous bearded ruffian would last against his superbly conditioned opponent.

Many figured the odds a hundred to one, and bets were placed on who would draw "first blood," on who would be knocked down first and how many rounds the fight might last.

The president at first obeyed the instructions of the referee, accepting the extended hand of his opponent.

But that's where the president's obeisance would end.

"You've heard the rules, now shake hands!" hollered the referee at the top of his lungs, to be heard above the furiously shouting mob. Fights had broken out in sections of the throng of onlookers, as money was placed in the hands of third parties – who disappeared into the milling mass of humanity, absconding with the cash.

The president's incognito appearances at bare knuckle exhibitions resulted often in chaos, manifested in the form of rioting if he was recognized. Once the president had made good his escape, he would be ruthlessly hunted by the enraged mobs. Men even vaguely resembling the POTUS were attacked viciously on the streets, being mistaken for the most hated president in United States history.

The beard, Johnson hoped, would prevent recognition, but if it didn't, he had Pinkerton and twenty armed security men placed carefully within the seething caldron of unruly, ill-bred spectators.

Bill Skinner glowered fiercely into the squinting eyes of the much smaller man who stood before him, extending his hand. Skinner was of a mind to cow the bearded man with his fierce glowering.

President Johnson grasped Skinner's hand in a strong handshake and did not let go. Instead, the president continued to squeeze, then in a sudden, violent, grinding motion – *BROKE IT!* He did not release the hand, but continued to grind it, feeling the splintered bones rub against one another.

The reaction from the larger man was immediate – he slapped Johnston hard across the left ear with his southpaw.

"YOU BASTARD!" shouted President Johnson, stepping back from Skinner and holding his left hand to his throbbing eardrum, which he thought may have been ruptured.

Skinner held up his right arm, bent at the elbow to shield his face as he advanced on the president. He took short, aimed jabs with his left hand at the much shorter, bearded man who backed away from him, with his hand to his ear. Skinner saw that his opponent could hardly stand and seemed to wobble and teeter – on the verge of falling down.

Johnson could hardly maintain his equilibrium and staggered drunkenly away from Skinner, who used his remaining hand in consummate skill born of thousands of fights.

"I'm going to finish you! I'm going to beat you to death!" remonstrated Skinner, missing with a powerful left round house that the president barely dodged.

"Stop talkin' and start chalkin'!" countered President Johnson, taking a short jab straight into the face. The blow tilted Johnson's head back violently and blood flew from the nose. Then a powerful roundhouse from Skinner's left hand connected solidly with the president's right jaw – sending him down.

"One! Two! Three..." the referee counted off as Johnson leaped from the floor of the ring onto his feet – this time like a man who has had an epiphany and is reborn.

"Round one ended! Each man to his corner!" shouted the referee. The combatants retired for a moment's respite to their respective corners before the bell sounded.

"Round two – *LET'S GET IT ON!!!*" announced the referee through cupped hands.

"That all you got?" Johnson taunted Skinner, who struck him again with another round house, causing sweat and blood to fly from Johnson's nose and hair.

"Show me what you got, Skinner! That right hand isn't doing you much good is it?" laughed Johnson. The president had begun to circle Skinner like a predator now, even though he was taking blows that would have fallen an ox.

Skinner launched a very powerful uppercut which almost carried him off balance. The president dodged, but still had not attempted to strike the larger man, although they were several minutes into the second round.

It was beginning to dawn on the champion that he was being taken measure of, by an experienced, dark horse opponent. Not only that but added to Skinner's concerns was his crushed right hand, which had swollen to twice its size.

Skinner launched a left hook which Johnson ducked. The president then drove into his opponent like a bull, driving him into one of the corner posts that supported the ropes.

Skinner grabbed for Johnson's beard in an attempt to rip it from his opponent's face, skin along with it. When the beard came off there was a collective gasp of surprise from the spectators.

"See what you've done?! *I was just beginning to enjoy myself!*" exclaimed Johnson.

Andrew Johnson realized that he would quickly be recognized for who he was. It was then that the most hated president in American history dug the thumb of his left hand into Skinner's right eye and tore it from the socket with an audible, "pop."

Wasting no time, the POTUS drove the fist of his powerful right arm into the taught abdomen of Skinner, doubling him over. The president continued, driving the heel of his cowboy boot into the back of his opponent's knee and sending him crashing to the floor.

"BREAK IT UP! STOP THE FIGHT!!! FOUL!!! IT'S A FOUL!!!" shouted the referee, pulling the determined President Johnson away from his defeated opponent.

"FOUL THIS!!!" expostulated the blood maddened president, who was enraged at having been

interrupted at the savage moment of climax. It seemed to the desperate referee that Johnson regarded him as the perpetrator of coitus interruptus as the president's right fist connected with his jaw.

The referee staggered backwards, his jaw disconnected from the vicious right hook that the president delivered. His shouting had ceased as he tried to work his dislocated jaw into place. He was shoved to the side as spectators entered the ring intent on attacking and doing physical harm to President Johnson.

"IT'S THE PRESIDENT!!! TO HIM!!! TAKE HIM DOWN!!!" shouted the enraged mob, seething and eddying as they attempted to enter the ring. The ropes of the ring bulged inward as the crowd pressed upon one another to enter the ring and attack the president.

"PARTY TIME!!!" responded President Johnson, as he dropped one attacker after another who swarmed into the ring to get him.

Suddenly gun shots rang out as Pinkerton men, led by Allen Pinkerton himself began shooting into the mob that was being obliterated by President Johnson. The crowd backed off seething in hate as the Irishmen and Scotsmen formed a human shield around the POTUS.

"MAKE A HOLE!!!" shouted President Johnson at the crowd of enraged attackers, laughing.

Then Johnson winked at Pinkerton, who acknowledged by ordering his men to:

"OPEN FIRE ON THEM – MAKE A HOLE FOR THE PRESIDENT!!!"

"That was a good cuff to the ear you gave me, Skinner," complimented the president, looking down at his opponent who raised his left arm in a plea for mercy. The president added, "Here, this is for you – good fight!" Johnson placed a twenty-dollar gold double eagle in the open hand of Skinner.

"Let's go to the train, Mr. President!" urged Allan Pinkerton, eager to be gone before the crowd regained their courage.

"Yeah! *I'm ready for a whiskey!!!*" agreed the POTUS, as they hurried to the presidential train with Pinkerton men gunning down everyone in their way. The steam locomotive was named, *"JUGGERNAUT."*

The table in the diner car was made of polished black walnut. On either side of it sat General Grant and President Johnson. On the table and between the two men sat an unopened bottle of Tennessee sipping whiskey.

The bottle was a flat sided, pear shaped vessel made of brown, translucent glass. It was popular during the time to feature the current president on the side of the glass and Johnson was on one side of the bottle - on the other side was a relief of the American Bald Eagle. The whiskey bottle was a short quart, also known as a "fifth."

The Commander in Chief raised the bottle to his mouth and broke the seal as he ripped the cork out with his strong, tobacco stained teeth.

As the train whistle let out a shrill cry to clear the protestors from the rail he tilted the bottle bottom side up.

Slowly, the train eased forward, urged by the powerful, inexorable thrust of the four-cylinder compound engine. The marvel of engineering was driven by saturated steam and propelled by fourteen-inch diameter pistons pumping on a sixteen-inch compression stroke. The smoke belching *JUGGERNAUT* was an iron colossus whose plow began to push through the throngs of humanity. In moments the plow shaped cattle guard of the *JUGGERNAUT* would hurl the protestors hundreds of feet to either side once it had gained momentum.

Air entered the bottle as the president swallowed with gusto, making rotund "blooping" sounds as air filled the vacuum and his Adam's apple bounced up and down.

"Ahhhhhhhhh! Nectar of the Gods, General Grant!" exclaimed President Johnson through split, swollen lips. The president wiped his mouth with the back of his powerful left hand. His shirt sleeves were pushed up above the elbows and exposed forearms thickly roped with sinewy muscles of steel. There must have been a total absence of fatty tissue beneath the skin, thought General Grant, because the muscle rippled and stood out boldly.

The POTUS sat the half-emptied bottle on the table and looked through eyes, nearly swollen shut, at the face of General Grant who sat directly across the table in front of him.

"That was a fight, now let me tell you! That Bill Skinner fought a better fight than you did," said the president, eyeing the cast on Grant's arm.

"Why did you bring me along?" asked General Grant, adding as an afterthought, "I signed the damned confession."

"Because I can't trust you," answered Johnson, adding, "you would foment insurrection – a coup d'état. You see, I was chosen by the Almighty to carry out His will, and I bear the marks of one who carries the Cross of suffering. I'm a Penitent. People malign me, lie about me, try to kill me…"

President Johnson once more digressed into a monolog of comparing himself emphatically to Christ. The powerful Tennessee bourbon loosened his tongue and eased the throbbing of the beating he'd taken at the hand of Skinner. That he had deliberately allowed the bare-knuckle champion to repeatedly strike him was in his mind a necessary act of penitence; an atonement.

But Johnson knew all along that he still controlled the fight and that gave rise to illusions of grandeur, in which Johnson saw himself as the suffering embodiment of the Messiah.

President Johnson pushed the half empty vessel toward his reticent guest and reached into a binder containing the daguerreotypes. His coal black, distrusting eyes fixed luridly on the images of the woman - like the eyes of a man who has gone mad.

"You are one sick puppy! What a pervert!!! Stealing my mail to look at naked pics!" the president suddenly, without warning shouted.

The POTUS grabbed the half empty bottle from Grant's mouth, finished it, and flung it across the diner car like a toddler flinging his pacifier.

"Hell no!!! None of that's true!!!" expostulated General Grant, feeling himself begin to anger at the false accusation. He angrily regarded the enigma of a man who sat before him.

"Doesn't matter," responded Johnson, adding, "you and I both are going to Fort Dodge to get things straightened out there. I will tell you exactly what to do, and you will, through your chain of command, see to it. The Cheyenne attacked in large numbers and nearly overtook the fort, and there is someone there who is very dear to my heart. This is all your doings."

Chapter Seventeen: Monahsetah

The attack on Fort Dodge, Kansas was unknown to the Yellow Hair as he completed the final details of evacuating his command from the burning village of Chief Black Kettle. The popping of unspent ammunition added a lethal intonation to the audible roar of the fires. The conflagrations consumed the tepees as a starving man consumes a plate of morsels. The orange-red flames seemed animated as though embodying demonic entities which danced like Roman candles a hundred feet and more into the arctic air.

The main body of 7th Cavalry was soon to be on the move. Preparations were hastily being completed when an explosion was heard and the ground shook as though from the detonation of an enormous stockpile of ammunition.

The glowing orb that lifted above the hills and sped toward the sky went almost unnoticed. The explosion was attributed to the detonation of a cache of ammunition, possibly a large store of dynamite.

Monahsetah, the daughter of Chief Little Rock, had been smitten and fallen in love with the Yellow Hair. She had been determined to marry Custer from the moment she saw him kill her father, Chief Little Rock; the co-chief of the doomed village of Chief Black Kettle.

The Boy General didn't have the sense of compassion that was necessary to feel the affection – the love at first sight that Monahsetah had immediately acquired for him. The Yellow Hair was completely oblivious to the woman who had been so open in the tepee with her natural appearance.

And now, a hawk faced, middle aged Cheyenne woman had placed a heavy buffalo coat over the figure of Monahsetah and brought the damsel to the Lieutenant Colonel.

Custer was issuing orders in hoarse, staccato bursts to his officers and paid no attention to what the older woman was saying in her native tongue. As an act of courtesy to his female prisoners he tolerated the placement of Monahsetah's hand into his. He wanted to convey the impression that no harm would befall them under his care.

When the former general stopped speaking he looked quizzically at the young woman holding his hand while the older woman began chanting. Despite all that was going on around him, he was oblivious to the extraneous stimuli that assailed his senses;

242

Custer was encapsulated in this pristine moment in time.

The older Cheyenne woman was hawkfaced and wore a parka-like coat made of buffalo skin, which was worn inside out so that the fur added insulation. The hood of the heavy coat was made of badger skin and the opening of the hood was lined with mink pelt.

Through the fur-lined opening of the hood the woman's lips urgently persisted with what to Custer seemed incantations; faster and faster she talked in her eerie, high toned, Algonquian Cheyenne dialect. The tonal pitch rose and fell, the woman was fairly shouting now above the wind.

Goose bumps arose on the arms of Custer, he felt his spine chill as the woman seemed to shout commands directed toward some atavistic deity.

He vaguely remembered superstitious tales of Indian witches recited to him by his long dead grandmother. Tales almost forgotten, bedtime stories told in the dark to instill fear in the boy as the wind wailed outside and tree branches scratched at his bedroom window.

The intonations that inflected the unbroken stream of words were ghostlike, paranormal and heavily nasal inflected.

Custer was becoming short of breath and his heart raced. He looked into the eyes of the witch-woman, who Custer knew, was aware that his consciousness was being visited.

The words spoken by the supernatural-like woman caused the azul eyes of Custer to regard her ever more analytically.

The lips of the enchantress appeared to be moving in slow motion now as the words rolled off her tongue in an unnaturally slow monotone, like a phonograph that is played backwards, very slowly.

She was, Custer thought, someone out of Hell who was casting an ominous spell; a spell which seemed to him in some remote part of his mind to originate from a time both pristine and primordial.

It was, he thought, as though he were at another place long ago in time – the situation being more akin to that of a distant hill people in the glacial age than of the present.

A freezing blast of wind caused the Boy General to shield his face. When he removed his hand, the woman was gone.

"What did she say?" Custer asked twenty-six-year-old Raphael Romero, an Army scout who had a Mexican father and an Arapaho mother.

Having been abducted at the age of nine by the Comanche and traded to the Kiowa and then other tribes, Romero spoke many of the languages that the Indians used, of which most were rooted in Algonquian.

Romero was of short stature and muscular, his bull neck supported a handsome, dark face that suggested his Spanish heritage. His jaw was strongly set, and his moustache was of the popular, grotesque walrus type.

"She was saying that you are husband to this maiden, General. She has married you to her. Your bride's name is Monahsetah," Romero answered Lt. Col. Custer.

Romero, like everyone else in the 7th Cavalry addressed Custer as "General," in deference to the temporary rank he had held during the Civil War.

The Boy General was shaken by the experience and was innately cognizant that those around him had in no way experienced what he had.

"Thomas," the Boy General addressed his younger brother, "have the bugler sound officers' call," Custer said, still shaking and not recovered from the supernatural experience. "for we are to leave this place forthwith,"

His sixth sense told him he was being watched, he turned about, locking his eyes onto the riveting, piercing stare of Monahsetah.

"Roger that, General," the two-time Medal of Honor recipient Thomas Custer replied. Thomas was the first soldier in history to receive the Medal of Honor twice.

Despite the rapidity with which the situation around him was developing, the Boy General could not help but to speculate upon his peculiar marital status; that of being married to a white woman and a Cheyenne woman concurrently.

Never being a religious man – not truly, he nevertheless considered the legal technicalities and possible ramifications on his career as a military officer in the Regular Army, where promotions were hard to come by.

Then too, he remembered the daguerreotypes. Anger, resentment, and the need for revenge steeled his heart.

"Bloody Knife – come here! On the double!" shouted Custer at a group of Indian Scouts who were frantically assisting prisoners onto their horses. Bloody Knife bolted from the group, double timing through the knee-deep snow toward the Yellow Hair.

"When we get back to the fort, I want you to kill a son of a bitch for me." Custer said to Bloody Knife.

There was the calm reassurance of knowing ahead of time that Bloody Knife would be glad to comply with the former general's wish that made the statement come across so casually.

"Bloody Knife kill!" responded the Arikawa enthusiastically.

"Good. When we get back to the fort, find the black man, Don L, and cut his throat," ordered Custer.

"Let it appear that "bad Injuns" did it. I know that you can be rather imaginative in that respect," the former general confided to Bloody Knife.
246

"Bloody Knife kill Don L for Boy General!" shouted Custer's favorite scout above the howling arctic wind.

"BLOODY KNIFE KILL!!!" reiterated the reliable, best friend of Custer. Then he returned to his fellow scouts and resumed preparations for departure.

"Now, what about you?" Custer asked softly, looking down at the diminutive, Romanesque beauty standing before him.

Her shoulders were narrow, and the neck strong and symmetrical – like that of a prima-ballerina. The neck supported a head that reflected the countenance of sanguine beauty. Her forehead was angled slightly back and emphasized the plucked eyebrows. The eyes were deep set liquid pools of jet, perfectly aligned and divided by a prominent nasal ridge. The cheeks were high set, and gold earrings dangled from either lobe. The nose was petite, and perfect. The lips were full, darkly pigmented with berry juice which complemented a small mouth with straight, white teeth.

Custer remembered vaguely that she was small breasted, and that her hips were pleasantly shaped. Beneath her buffalo skin winter coat, she wore a dress adorned with magical icons and embellished with brass. Her necklaces consisted of bear claws and human teeth. Beaten copper rings and bracelets adorned her fingers and wrists.

"Let me fix that coat for you," the Yellow Hair added thoughtfully, tenderly, tightening a belt made of thin rope and adjusting the fit of the buffalo coat.

His kind words were no sooner spoken than they vanished in the split second that it took for the howling wind to carry them away.

The lieutenant colonel stood stupefied, looking down at Monahsetah's hand, as she rubbed herself, staring the Boy General fiercely into the eye...

About the Author

I'm William (Bill) Sumrall, born in Florida back in 1959.

A biography, such a simple word, but when one is faced with describing his own life it becomes less simple. Complicated is a better word. As a young man I took a BA in Spanish. I was a sergeant in a Marine Rifle Company. Also, I have a wide array of interests and hobbies, the latest being a popular game called "Trivia Crack."

I married at age thirty to my wife Maria and we have two adult children; daughter Kyla in the Navy, and son Billy in the Army.

I work in a rural hospital in Oklahoma.

Writing escapist historical fiction has given me a lot of laughs. I hope nobody gets too bent out of shape with my portrayal of the Weird West.

More by William Sumrall:

Metal Storm: Weird Custer

Warface! Weird Custer